I felt familiar butterflies in my stomach.

This usually happened when I was around my cousin Courtney and when she was about to get us into trouble again. It didn't make sense now, because Courtney—or my crazy cousin Courtney, as I still thought of her sometimes—was supposed to be reformed. She was coming back to New York City to play a part in a made-for-television movie, *The Laundry Bag Murder.* She was going to be a movie star at the age of thirteen!

Books by Judi Miller

My Crazy Cousin Courtney
My Crazy Cousin Courtney Comes Back
My Crazy Cousin Courtney Returns Again

Available from MINSTREL Books

RETURNS AGAIN

Judi Miller

PUBLISHED BY POCKET BOOKS

New York   London   Toronto   Sydney   Tokyo   Singapore

This book is a work of fiction. Names, characters, places, and incidents are products of the author's imagination or are used fictitiously. Any resemblance to actual events or locales or persons, living or dead, is entirely coincidental.

A MINSTREL PAPERBACK *Original*

 A Minstrel Book published by
POCKET BOOKS, a division of Simon & Schuster Inc.
1230 Avenue of the Americas, New York, NY 10020

Copyright © 1995 by Judi Miller

All rights reserved, including the right to reproduce this book or portions thereof in any form whatsoever. For information address Pocket Books, 1230 Avenue of the Americas, New York, NY 10020

ISBN: 0-671-88733-5

First Minstrel Books printing March 1995

10 9 8 7 6 5 4 3 2

A MINSTREL BOOK and colophon are registered trademarks of Simon & Schuster Inc.

Cover art by Carla Dagwan/Sormanti

Printed in the U.S.A.

for my cousins, Megan and Matthew

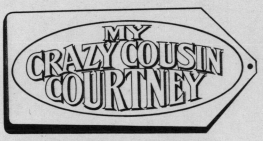

RETURNS AGAIN

June 16

Dear Courtney,

(Or should I call you Tiffany from now on?)

I can't believe it! You're actually coming back to stay with us in New York City in two weeks! You're really, really coming back, and to shoot a movie. You must be thrilled! Felicity and Dawn were dying to meet you because they never met a real live movie star and because you're my cousin. But Felicity is going to visit her aunt in Ireland, and Dawn is spending the summer with her cousins in Cincinnati.

Yesterday was the first day at Camp Acorn. Frank is back, of course, and so are Laverne and

1

Latoya. Zora Zimmerman is writing a new book, *Be Still My Heart.*

Phyllis's New Zoo finally opened and last night I had to go with my mom to the airport to pick up a real live gorilla from Africa. We had to put him on another flight for South America, where he's going to star in a movie. Some lady saw him in his cage and almost fainted. I thought he looked harmless and kind of cute.

His name was Melvyn, but his stage name was Son of King Kong. Am I writing too much? I always write too much. Pretty soon we'll be picking you—a movie star—up at the airport! Well, I have to run. Howard is taking us to Hung Lo's for Chinese food. See you soon!

Love and loads of hugs and kisses and to Wilheim Von Dog, too.

Cathy

Is it Friday so soon?

My darling cousin Cathy,

It was divine hearing from you.

Bernie and Joan said when I finish working

on the made-for-television movie I have to go back to work, for free, at Camp Acorn.

I was aghast, but I shall have to make the best of it.

Well, I must rehearse.

Luv,
Tiffany

CHAPTER ONE

I felt familiar butterflies in my stomach.

This usually happened when I was around my cousin Courtney and when she was about to get us into trouble again. It didn't make sense now because Courtney, or my crazy cousin Courtney, as I still thought of her sometimes, was supposed to be reformed. She was coming back to New York City to play a part in a made-for-television movie, *The Laundry Bag Murder*. She was going to be a movie star at the age of thirteen!

But she was also nowhere to be found at mammoth JFK International Airport in New York City. It seemed she hadn't landed with the plane.

My mom, her husband Howard, Frank, and his grandmother, Mrs. Phillips, who is also Courtney's agent, and I were all clustered near the baggage carousel where Courtney was supposed to meet us. Everyone was searching frantically. Courtney's plane from Los Angeles International Airport had supposedly landed at twelve thirty-six. Now it was seven minutes till two and we were still looking for Courtney.

Frank put his hand on my arm and said gently, "Don't worry, Cath. She'll turn up."

I nodded numbly. I knew Courtney wouldn't miss coming to New York to be in her movie for the world. So where was she? What if she got lost, hopped on the wrong plane, couldn't find her dog, Wilheim Von Dog? What if she was in trouble?

As far as getting into trouble, Courtney was capable of anything just in the general course of the day.

That's what I loved about her. She was fun. Sometimes too much fun, but fun.

Suddenly my mom shouted, "Oh, look, there she is!" We all spun around as Mom rushed to embrace a very pretty girl with strawberry blond hair. "Courtney!" my mom shouted, hugging her from behind.

The girl turned around, shocked.

"My name is Cheryl," she announced in perfectly articulated tones.

My mom shrank back, embarrassed.

6

Mrs. Phillips checked her watch and then said worriedly, "Maybe we should have her paged."

"Maybe we should go to the Lost and Found," I suggested.

"Oh, she'll be here," Howard assured us. Howard and my mom had gotten married in September. He was very relaxed and always took us out for Chinese food. "She probably wants to make an entrance."

I suddenly got a picture of Courtney hiding in the ladies' room until just the right moment. Come to think of it, Howard could be right. Courtney's last letter had been, well, kind of odd. She wrote as if she were playing a great tragic role when all she was really playing was a thirteen-year-old kid in a made-for-television mystery. Of course it was every kid's dream who wanted to be a movie star. Me, I wanted to be a writer.

I had been waiting since January for Courtney to come to stay with us again. Today was the day.

Except she wasn't here.

My mom, frantic in the way only she can get, spotted another girl who resembled Courtney.

"Courtney!" Mom screamed before we could hold her back.

The girl raised her head as my mom, her honey-colored hair flying out of her hair clip, ran toward her.

"My name's Agatha," the girl said. "But Courtney's a nice name."

7

"Maybe one of us should call her home in Beverly Hills to see if something went wrong, if maybe there was an accident or something," Mrs. Phillips said, running out of words. My crazy cousin Courtney was a bit of a legend. Howard was nominated to make the phone call while we all waited.

One nagging question kept eating away at me. Why pull a stunt now? Now, when she had it all? She didn't even have to wait until she was sixteen to change her name to Tiffany.

To think that Courtney might have pulled a stunt like this for publicity was preposterous, I tried to convince myself. Not when five people were waiting for her. Even Courtney couldn't do that. Could she? Then I began to feel guilty for thinking she would when something was obviously wrong. I guess like Courtney said, I always think everything's my fault.

My mom spotted a girl with sunglasses who really did look like Courtney. She even had *me* fooled. My mom ran over to her and threw her arms around the girl. The girl shut her eyes, her arms tight to her sides, and, without smiling said, "And they say New Yorkers aren't friendly."

While we waited for Howard to play dodge'em through the crowds, I kept watching for Courtney or her six pieces of luggage to go around the carousel. Or maybe there would be twelve pieces and a foot locker now that she was this big movie star.

One good thing was that Courtney would be working

8

all day and we wouldn't have time to get in trouble. Probably. But then I felt that creepy sensation again. My butterflies. It wasn't only that I was afraid Courtney was lost, but I also wondered when she did turn up if she'd be a different Courtney. She might be too sophisticated to bother with me. She would be with movie people all day and we'd have nothing in common.

I'd almost rather we got into trouble all the time than that. Because then at least Courtney had been fun and not a snob! Then I realized I had been daydreaming. Courtney hadn't even arrived yet.

Howard located our little cluster and shook his head. "No luck," he said. "All I got was an answering machine."

I checked my watch again. The second hand had jumped a minute. The baggage carousel had only one piece of luggage going round and round, and I knew it didn't belong to Courtney.

Then I heard a piercing scream.

At first none of us could tell where it was coming from.

"Look, look over there," Howard said, shielding his eyes as if the sun were blazing.

Then I saw her—my crazy cousin Courtney!

She was riding on the back of one of those luggage trucks and waving like she was the President of the United States—or the First Lady. Her suitcases, all of them, were neatly piled around her, one on top of the other. It had probably taken a while to figure out which one went where. In back of her was another little truck with more luggage that obviously belonged to her. I could see her foot locker sticking out.

This was Courtney all right! She had on her trademark heart-shaped red-sequined sunglasses and a fur jacket. Of course, knowing Courtney, it was a very fancy fake fur jacket because she loved animals too much to wear them. From where we were standing, still grouped around the baggage carousel, it looked as if she were swathed in mink, though.

Courtney was making an entrance, planned or not.

She sure had a lot of luggage. More than last year when she came to visit us, but this year my mom and Howard and I had moved into a large co-op apartment and we had more room, which was good because Courtney had brought more clothes. Though last year she had never unpacked the ones she brought—not until right before she went home.

Courtney was still waving as the driver inched closer.

"Don't worry, Cath," Frank said, standing at my side. He touched my arm and I felt tingly all over. Good old Frank. Somehow he knew I wasn't sure Courtney would be, well, the Courtney we all knew and loved.

I knew Frank understood and I wanted to reach up and touch that lock of wayward sandy hair that had fallen onto his perfect golden tan forehead. I was worried we would lose Courtney when she became a movie star. I didn't want to lose her, because even as we bailed her out of trouble, we knew what a good kid she was.

I'd hate to see her change, but then I hated to see anything change. I wanted everything to stay the same. I was still getting used to the fact that, at Christmas, Frank told me he liked me and not Courtney.

I watched as Courtney slowly stepped from the truck holding the hand of the driver. She was wearing little heels and skinny pants. Finally my cousin Courtney was here! I had been waiting for this moment for months!

Would she still be Courtney? My very best friend and second cousin all rolled into one?

We waved. Then all at once she was rushing toward us, a big purple bubble replacing her face. My mom shouted, "Courtney!" and rushed to hug her. They kissed and as my mom was picking purple bubble gum off her mouth she said, "Where were you? We've been here for hours. Are you all right?"

"I'm sorry. I missed my flight and had to take another one. I got all my luggage as fast as I could and came over here to meet you."

"Well, I'm just glad you're here, Courtney. Or should I call you Tiffany?" Mom asked.

"No," Courtney replied almost gravely. "Bernie

11

says I'm only Tiffany when I'm on the movie. The rest of the time I'm Courtney. This is Wilheim Von Dog. He's a Bee-Shawn Free-zay. It's spelled B-I-C-H-O-N F-R-I-S-E with a slanty accent over the *E*."

My mom immediately turned into melted butter over this white ball of fluff with the coal-black paws, eyes, and nose.

My mom had the biggest, well, actually, the only animal theatrical agency in town. "Phyllis's New Zoo." The first one had closed down because the building it was in was condemned. She then managed people for a while with Mrs. Phillips, Frank's grandmother, but now she an own animal agency again because that's what she loved to do.

Courtney took off her jacket right then and revealed a T-shirt that announced "The Middle Initial in My Name Is *O* for *Outrageous.*" Then she turned toward me.

She uttered another piercing scream that caused some travelers to snap their heads around, others to lose the grip on their luggage anticipating terrorist trouble, at the very least, and others to look her way just because, well, she was so pretty.

"Oh, my God!" she shrieked. "Cathy, you got your hair cut!"

CHAPTER TWO

"Turn around!" Courtney squealed at me.

I turned around.

The long single braid that had hung down my back since the age of eight (before that I had worn my hair in two long braids) was gone. Now I had hair that stopped just below my shoulders. Of course it wasn't perfect like Courtney's naturally curly hair.

Courtney glanced at Frank and nudged me with her elbow, winking like she had something in her eye. I knew what she was thinking—that I had cut my hair to impress Frank. But I wouldn't do that. I had cut it because I was ready.

Hadn't I?

"Would you believe I haven't got a thing to wear?" Courtney said melodramatically as Frank and Howard struggled to get her luggage out. We ended up taking three cabs to our new apartment house, which was two blocks away from our old apartment house. The doorman, Murray, looked as if he were somewhere between having a massive heart attack and anticipating a huge tip for Christmas when he saw Courtney's luggage. He did help us load it into the elevator.

We ended up shoving everything in the guest room. Courtney was going to sleep in the room my mom had decorated for me with pink and white twin beds and a vanity table.

"Anybody hungry?" Howard asked all of us. We were all starving, so Howard took us to Hung Lo's, the Chinese restaurant where he and my mom had had their wedding reception. I couldn't help but notice how everyone turned to stare at Courtney on the street. She had really bloomed. Her rich strawberry blond hair twisted into neat little curls; her misty blue-green eyes changed and became vibrant in the sunlight. Her peaches-and-cream complexion would never need makeup. Courtney never wore anything but a smudge of green eye shadow to match her eyes, the ever-present pistachio-pink nail polish, and every once in a while, for effect, a slash of juicy orange lipstick. She was utterly gorgeous. That's why a lot

14

of girls didn't like her. However, she had lots of friends who were boys.

When we got there, Mr. Hung Lo, himself, came over to our table, with the menus, and I introduced Courtney.

"This is my cousin Courtney from Beverly Hills, California. She's visiting us for the summer and also she's a movie star."

Mr. Lo bowed. "A movie star? Well, you will have to autograph a picture and send it to me and I will put it in the window along with the other pictures of big stars who do Hung Lo's an honor by dining here."

Mrs. Phillips, Courtney's agent, smiled. "I'll have my secretary send you one tomorrow."

Instead Courtney whipped out an eight-by-ten glossy photo of herself and a pen from her oversize bag. She sucked on the pen tip as she wondered how to autograph it.

I couldn't believe it.

When I visited her in Beverly Hills, all we did was chase stars for autographs (and get into trouble). Now here she was giving an autograph, and she hadn't even started to work yet! I watched as she signed her photo "Tiffany Green" in big, sprawling letters. It was a nice picture of her holding Wilheim Von Dog, who was wearing a black bow to match her black dress.

After dinner Courtney peeled open every fortune

15

cookie—she was choosing the fortune she liked best. Then we went home. Courtney and I ended up plopping down on the two pink and white twin beds. She opened up a fresh piece of bubble gum and offered me one.

"Lemon Twist," she said.

Then we just lay there like two beached whales blowing bubbles and popping them. It must have sounded like someone popping balloons at a party.

"So, Cathy," Courtney said, lying flat on her back. "How is everything going in the Frank department?"

I could immediately feel my face begin to get hot. That's what happens when I blush. Next my ears get pink. That's the dead giveaway then.

"Why do you ask?" I said quietly.

She accidentally swallowed her bubble gum and had to get another piece.

"Oh, I don't know. You just don't act like boyfriend and girlfriend," she blurted out.

What could I say to my sophisticated, savvy cousin Courtney who had just arrived from glittery Beverly Hills? That Frank had arrived a week ago from Idaho, we had both resumed our jobs as camp counselors at Camp Acorn, and everything was just like last year except we were minus Courtney. I had written him two letters over the last six months. He had written me one, which I had pasted into my scrap-

16

book. But face to face, he was shy and I was shy. There was nothing doing even though he had asked me to be his girlfriend at Christmas. But I didn't want to admit it to Courtney. She was so good with boys.

"So nothin's happening, huh?" Courtney said, popping a bubble. I waited until she lifted the gum off her face.

"Uh-uh," I said. "He's nice to me, but then after camp every afternoon he says he's tired and goes home to watch TV and have a soda."

She nodded seriously. "Maybe he says that, but maybe he doesn't really know what to do. But I think he really likes you—a lot—Cath."

That made it worse because I, who could never figure out boys anyway, felt even less confident now.

"I've got it!" Courtney screeched. "Let's role play!"

"Oh, no," I said, shaking my head. "I couldn't. We just ate."

"Role play, Cathy. It's when you rehearse a situation before you do it. I found it in an acting book. Salespeople train with this all the time. You be Frank and I'll be you and we'll talk, and that way you can be used to having a deep discussion with him."

"Okay," I said a little reluctantly, thinking at the time that this was better than trying to rescue my

17

crazy cousin Courtney before she fell off the top of the Empire State Building or something.

"So, Frank, nice weather we've been having. Though they say we might see some scattered showers by Tuesday."

"Courtney!" I exploded nervously. "That's *not* a deep discussion!"

"Wait a second, wait a second. I was just warming up. So, Frank, how about coming over after work? I have some soda. There's a TV. We can just hang out for a while."

"Courtney! I can't ask him that. That's like asking him out for a date!"

"Well, it's more like asking him in. So that's not asking him out. It's not as if you're asking him out on a date!"

"Is, too!"

"Is not!"

"Too!"

"Not!"

"Too!"

Just then we looked up and I saw my mother standing in the doorway wearing the pretty rose-colored quilted bathrobe Courtney's mother Joan had sent her for Christmas. "Girls," she said. "I thought I heard you fighting just now. Not on Courtney's first night. Go to sleep early. We all have to go to work tomorrow."

She shut the door. Courtney started to giggle and

18

hid her head somewhere between the pillow and the pillowcase. I started to giggle, too, and ducked under the covers. But there was something juicy about Courtney's giggle. It was infectious. They should put it in a bottle and package it in the supermarkets. Maybe she could win the Emmy for Best Giggler. It always took a while for Courtney to stop and catch her breath.

"Okay, let's go back to role playing," she said.

"Oh, I don't think it will work, Courtney," I said. "I mean, role playing may be a good way to sell houses and act in plays, but I don't think it works to get a boyfriend."

She nodded. Sometimes with Courtney you couldn't tell if she was nodding or shaking her head no. She was stroking Wilheim Von Dog, who was staring up at me intensely with his coal-black eyes peeking out of his fluffy white body.

"I've got it!" she shrieked.

"What, Courtney? What do you have?"

She was still for a minute, and I could tell her thought processes were whizzing. Courtney had the attention span of a six-month-old infant most of the time. But not when it came to boys.

Then she said simply, "I forgot."

"Oh," I said, sinking back on the pillow.

She shot up. "No, I remember. You see, what you have to do, Cathy, is act a little more helpless. You're too competent."

A little more helpless. Gee, I didn't think I was helpless at all.

"You're too practical and down to earth," Courtney was saying. "Of course, that's why Frank likes you because he's the same way." But I had tuned her out. The butterflies were back, and it wasn't the shrimp with lobster sauce. It was Courtney. Anyway she could do it she would involve me in an adventure.

"I've got it! The next time you have a chance to talk to Frank, really talk, tell him—tell him someone's following you."

I had to stop her. "Courtney, that's crazy."

"No, it isn't. Listen, I know Frank. He'll want to protect you, take care of you, walk you home, buy you a soda."

I saw the way her wheels were spinning. But why would anyone be following me? As much as I hated to admit it—even though Courtney might be off the wall on everything else—she was an expert on boys. She couldn't even count her boyfriends on both hands and Frank was only my first kind-of boyfriend. It might take awhile—like the whole summer—for us to get comfortable with each other. But our relationship wouldn't be based on a lie.

"Courtney," I finally said. "I can't tell a lie. I can't tell Frank someone is following me."

"But, Cathy, just say I *think* someone's following me. That's not a lie."

20

Maybe she was right. Maybe this would speed everything up.

"Courtney," I said after we had undressed and were under the covers.

"Courtney?" I asked.

She had fallen asleep and we hadn't worked out the details.

CHAPTER
THREE

Courtney had had Joan, who's Courtney's mom, buy her some books on acting back home in Beverly Hills. She really wanted to become a serious actress and told me she was swearing off boys. (Of course, that was hard to believe!) But to be a movie star at thirteen—was more than any girl could want!

Except me. I wanted to be a writer.

And I had Frank now—sort of. What more could I want?

After work one day Frank and I went to watch Courtney when the film started shooting. It was late afternoon out-of-doors on a shady tree-lined street in Greenwich Village. All the dog-walkers had stopped to watch with Frank and me. We were across the street from the action, next to the big lights.

I was so proud of Courtney.

She was wearing a kelly-green velvet top and black skinny pants. Even from across the street the top made her green-blue eyes look as green as shamrocks and her reddish curls like a cluster of coppery pennies.

"I heard it with my own eyes," Courtney said very dramatically and stopped abruptly.

Clint Carothers, the very handsome blond director, rushed up and placed his hands on her shoulders.

"It's—'I heard it with my own ears, dear'—now don't get nervous, you're doing beautifully, beautifully."

Courtney nodded. When they said "Action" again she had to cry. She really cried professionally. I believed her. The officer asked her on what floor the murder had taken place. She shook her head and kept on crying. A lady next to us took out a Kleenex.

Courtney was now sobbing uncontrollably. She was really good at it. Especially since she had to start and stop on cue. I asked her the day before if she needed an onion to cry. She said, no, she had found something in her acting book that was better.

"You think of something sad," she said to me, her green-blue eyes clouding over.

23

"But what could you think of?" I asked her. She had everything.

"Something bad happening to Wilheim Von Dog."
I nodded.

"He could be run over by a Rolls-Royce; he could be kidnapped for ransom; he could run off with a poodle."

I saw what she meant.

Pretty soon I was crying with her.

My mother appeared in the doorway.

"Anything wrong, girls?"

We shook our heads and kept crying. "It's Wilheim Von Dog."

My mother got alarmed. She had grown just as attached to him as Courtney, almost.

"No, Phyllis, relax," Courtney said, shaking her coppery curls as if she were shaking moonbeams out of her hair. "It's just an acting trick."

My mom was relieved. She couldn't bear to have anything bad happen to animals. Not just dogs. Foxes, bears, giraffes, elephants—she loved all animals.

I then saw Courtney giving us a secret little wave. I could see she was excited. Courtney loved crowds. And she gathered one every time we got into trouble, which was a lot.

I was just so happy for her. She had exactly what she wanted—she was Tiffany Courtney Alicia Green.

Thirteen-year-old movie star. And I think I had what I wanted. Frank Phillips, from Idaho, a little on the shy side. Now what did I do? I could do what Courtney advised me to do and in a helpless southern belle accent tell him—"Fraaaaank, Ah do belieeeve someone's following me." Of course it could be a mugger or someone who wanted to lift my watch or a long-lost friend from the Girl Scouts. Was that a lie?

Or I could spend the summer trying to bring out a fifteen-year-old—well, almost fifteen-year-old boy—who retreated every day behind a frosty glass of soda to the talk shows on TV. Or I could ask him in, which still seemed to me like asking him out if he didn't ask me out before I asked him in. Of course, I wasn't as clever with boys as Courtney was.

Courtney made a gesture to me between takes. She had seen us. She pointed at Frank and then she appeared frantic.

Frank looked down at me, puzzled.

"Anything wrong?"

I shook my head. "No, you know Courtney. She just talks a lot, with or without her hands." I did know what she was trying to tell me to do. Tell Frank that someone was following me and do it *now!*

Courtney did everything *now*.

Actually, I did have to do it now because Courtney wasn't shooting the next day. That meant she would come to Camp Acorn with us and be a movie star turned camp counselor. If I didn't tell him she'd never let me have any peace the whole day.

I just had to think of a way to do it so it wouldn't seem as if I was lying. It was almost physically impossible for me to tell a lie. Once when I was eight I told a lie and my mom found out and I ended up with this horrible rash.

Courtney could tell a lie. In fact, she did all the time. But she did it by telling herself it was a little white lie. It was for the other person's own good. Or she would cross her fingers behind her back. Or she would twist everything around so it sounded almost like a half-truth.

But I wasn't Courtney. And this was a whopper.

I decided to get it over quickly—like ripping off a Band-Aid. It hurt less that way in the long run.

"Frank," I blurted out. "I think someone's following me."

"What?" he said.

"I think someone's following me." I think then I could have done a better job of fake crying than Courtney. The thing about lies is they build and build until they become a house of cards. If you pull one card out the whole thing comes tumbling down and then you're branded a liar for the rest of your life— if they don't send you to jail.

"Wow," Frank said, quickly turning around.

"No, don't turn now," I said dramatically as if

Courtney had stepped inside my body and was operating my vocal cords.

He shook his head.

"I mean if this was anyone else"—(meaning a certain person called my crazy cousin Courtney, whom it really was)—"I would wonder about this, but not from you, Cath. You're so down to earth, so solid, so matter-of-fact."

My ears turned pink. That's not what I wanted to be. I wanted to be—just a little, not a lot—like my cousin Courtney standing there in her kelly-green top and her coppery curls. I couldn't figure out if he was complimenting me or not.

"Are you sure, Cathy?"

I nodded, but in my mind I was shaking my head. Since Frank had become my boyfriend, in name only, I wasn't sure of anything anymore.

"Is it a man or a woman?" I forgot Frank was into detective stories.

We hadn't thought that far. You can't tell a lie or a half-lie if it doesn't make sense. On the other other hand, I had once heard that if you're going to lie— keep it simple.

I said simply, "I don't know. He or she stays back at a distance. Sometimes I see him or her and sometimes I don't."

"When did this start?"

Why did Courtney do these things to me? Even

27

when she wasn't right beside me, she got me into trouble.

"I'm not sure," I said.

"You poor kid," Frank said. Great, now I was this poor kid. But then he put his arm around me and took my hand in his. Of course it was for all the wrong reasons, but it did happen.

"Cathy," he said gravely, "I know you. If you say someone's following you, it's serious. Don't worry. I'll take care of you. I'll stick right to you."

My ears turned pink. Where would this end? And the part about taking care of me. But he would be beside me—like a bodyguard. And his hand felt so warm and right in mine that suddenly I said, "Frank, do you want to come to my apartment for a root beer or something?"

He nodded and smiled, and his hand in mine, we headed toward my apartment.

I did it. Wait until I told Courtney. I had actually asked him out or "in" for a date and broken the ice. Courtney sure knew a lot about boys.

When we got to my apartment, Howard was there working with his ever-present calculator. He stopped to talk to Frank about whether the Mets would beat the Cleveland Indians when I went into the kitchen to get our sodas.

My mom was talking on the phone in the kitchen. "Sweetheart, I can only give you until seven o'clock. If Jolly the Giraffe doesn't take the part, they'll give it to an elephant who's a nobody. Two thousand dollars is my limit, and I don't care if the Bronx Zoo wanted her first!" My mom slammed down the phone and I could see how happy she was. She was doing what she loved. And she was great at it! I was proud of my mom. She was gutsy. I wasn't so sure I was.

"So, how are things in the Frank department?" my mother said.

"Oh, he's sitting in the living room, and I'm getting us root beer," I answered.

"Well, well," she said, smiling.

I wanted to say more, but I couldn't. How could I say to a woman who had single-handedly built the only animal theatrical agency in town that I had lied to get a boyfriend to pay attention to me?

I wanted to tell her he held my hand, but I couldn't because I had tricked him. All I could say was, "Everything's fine, Mom. The ice cubes are melting."

As I went in with the sodas, Frank looked up at me and smiled and my heart melted.

Maybe Courtney was right this time.

CHAPTER——
——FOUR

T he next morning Courtney was ready bright and early and wearing her new regulation T-shirt that said Camp Acorn, red shorts, white sneaks, and red socks. Around her neck was a long cord with a ballpoint pen dangling from it, just in case any kid wanted her autograph. I was so proud of her.

When we got to work, Zora Zimmerman cooed, "Do you know who this is, children?" She had her arms on Courtney's shoulders.

Twenty-four little kids with curious upturned faces sat cross-legged on the floor staring up at us.

No one said anything.

Finally Kevin, one little boy who had been there

last year, said, "I remember who she is. They're cousins. That's the other one."

Zora said, "That's right, Kevin. This is Courtney. She's visiting us for the day. Do you know who she really is?"

No one said anything.

"Courtney is a movie star. She's filming a made-for-television movie right here in New York. And here's the best part—when she's finished shooting her movie, she's going to join Cathy and Frank and Laverne and Latoya as a counselor here at Camp Acorn. This is the first time we've had a real live movie star as a counselor."

There was silence for a moment, and then one little girl squeaked, "Do you know Macaulay Culkin?"

"No, but I have his autograph," Courtney replied.

"When did you start becoming a movie star?" one little boy asked suspiciously. "I've never seen you in the movies or on television. Do you do commercials?"

"Children, children," Zora Zimmerman said, clapping her hands. She was wearing a bright orange and yellow caftan that resembled a sunrise. "This is Courtney's first movie, and she is a good example of what you can do if you try very hard."

I thought about that. Courtney hadn't tried at all. Everything just came to Courtney. Except, of course, good grades.

Then all the kids got up to get their lunch bags

and to pluck their subway tokens from a basket. Zora had switched to making Swiss cheese sandwiches because at the end of last summer there had been a peanut butter and jelly revolution. Peanut butter and jelly had gotten monotonous.

Zora Zimmerman's Camp Acorn was as unique as she was. The camp was held in her spacious loft apartment, which was light and cheery and had highly polished wooden floors. The kids played there and did crafts on rainy days.

Zora had a closetlike office with papers scattered all over where she worked. She was a published author. I had never met one before. She wrote romance novels. Last summer she had been working on *Sweet Reckless Love.* On a fresh, sunshiny day when we went outdoors she would sit quietly and churn out pages. On a good day when she wrote fifteen pages or more she would pass out homemade oatmeal-raisin cookies.

When it was nice out we took all the kids—paired off in buddies, so we would be able to keep track of them—to city pools, to Central Park to play softball and have picnics and ride the carousel, to the Bronx Zoo, to Coney Island, even to museums. New York could be a lot of fun in the summer. But being a counselor was exhausting work. No wonder Frank just wanted a glass of iced soda and a warm TV at night. He did most of the work.

That day we buddied the kids off, trouped them

down in the subway station at Seventy-ninth Street, and watched as they plunked in their tokens and passed through the turnstile. Some passengers on the train crossed into another car when they saw all our kids coming, but most people stared at us, bemused, because the sight of twenty-four little kids, holding on to the poles and one another, clutching paper lunch bags, was adorable. But not to us. But we had to keep track of them and make sure they weren't pushing one another or screaming or crying or somehow making the other passengers want to stick their fists in the kids' mouths.

It was when I was blowing Julianna's nose that I noticed a lady staring. She wasn't staring at the kids who were jumping around climbing the steel poles and singing camp songs. She was staring straight at me. She had pale blond hair pulled back in a low ponytail, white framed sunglasses that had slipped to the tip of her nose, and a large white straw hat. She was reading a Chinese newspaper. As soon as I spotted her, she buried her face in the paper. But one thing I was positive of about her was that she was definitely interested in me. She really could be following me. But that was crazy. I'd have to think this over. I must have made a mistake. Sure, I made a mistake.

Our Camp Acorn Excursion, as Zora called it, was to the Carmine Street Pool on LeRoy Street right near the branch of the library I especially liked to visit. We had been to the pool there last year. Admission was free after June, but Zora had special arrangements with a lot of other places in New York so we got in at reduced rates or free most places.

There was now so much noise and confusion with the kids that I forgot about the strange lady with the obvious disguise, and I wasn't going to remember it until much later.

Zora was a firm believer in physical fitness, and in New York that meant walking, so we got out at the subway stop early and with all the little kids squinting into the bright sunshine started walking toward Bleeker Street, which was a long street in Greenwich Village. We passed a store with parrots in the window and a Chinese restaurant and a bakery with yummy-looking whipped-cream cakes. Then we turned right and passed a locksmith, a newly opened café, and, of course, the library. Walking was really good exercise, and I noticed Courtney was enjoying it. I couldn't believe the change in her. No trouble, no boys. She was making me nervous.

At the entrance to the pool we counted the kids again and made sure no one had forgotten his or her bathing suit. The idea was to take a swim first since the kids couldn't swim for an hour after they ate. By lunchtime the Swiss cheese would be all melty, which was the way the kids said they liked it. Kind of like a sauceless pizza.

Eight little boys went with Frank to change and

sixteen little girls went with Courtney, Latoya, Laverne, and myself. I noticed when all twenty-four kids got out into the pool area, two ladies picked up the towels they had been sunbathing on and vanished.

In a way I didn't blame them.

City pools could really get crowded, so we all had to concentrate on keeping track of the kids and be there if they stubbed toes and encourage them to swim and stop them from splashing other little kids. Especially if the kid getting splashed wasn't one of the kids in your group.

Before we were all assembled, Courtney had dashed to the edge of the middle of the pool and put her hands together over her head ready to plunge right into the pool. She bellyflopped and made such a giant splash that everyone else stopped splashing.

All I could see was a streak of hot pink and orangey bikini as she swam expertly to the far side. The lifeguard gave her his undivided attention, though it was not because she was in any danger but because she just looked so beautiful. Then, in very Courtney-like fashion, she gracefully boosted herself out of the pool and shook out her wet hair like a dog shaking out his glistening fur. The noise level in the pool, which had temporarily diminished, came back until I almost wished I had earplugs.

It was a good thing Courtney took her dip early because we had twenty-four rambunctious kids who all wanted to take theirs. Frank, Laverne, and Latoya took charge of most of them. Courtney helped by giving the swimming lessons. Laverne and Latoya were in charge of calling kids with blue lips out of the water and making sure they got some sun. I had the little kids who were staying in the two- and three-foot section. I wasn't a great swimmer. I could dog-paddle, though.

I was watching the kids, but out of the corner of my eye I was studying Frank. All of the kids adored Frank. It occurred to me again what a terrific father he'd make. This was odd because of what he said of his home life. His own father wasn't terrific, which was why Frank usually stayed with his grandmothers during vacations. He had such a gentle, humorous way with the kids, and they obviously worshipped him. I got even more of a crush on him.

Sometimes when I was around Frank I tried to remember my own father, but I always blocked. I was young when he and my mom got divorced.

Just then Laverne boosted a little girl out of the pool.

"Blue lips," she said to me as if she were accusing the child of a crime.

The little girl's teeth were chattering, but she kept repeating, "Wanna go back in the water."

Courtney was holding a little boy under the stomach, and he was practicing his kick and his stroke. Boy, Courtney sure had changed. Being a movie star had done wonders for her—and me. She didn't need to get into trouble anymore to have fun. Though I still had a feeling that trouble followed her.

Right then out of the blue I recalled the blond Mystery Woman from the subway. I suddenly felt cold and figured I must have blue lips, too. The pool became icy and the sun disappeared behind a cloud. But this wasn't the right time to tell Courtney or Frank about her, because they were too busy.

With twenty-four kids ranging in age from six to nine, we were kept hopping. Zora's two kids attended the camp, also. I'd like to say they were well behaved, but they usually set a bad example for the rest of the campers. They believed they had been Native Americans in another life and did rain dances and tried to light campfires—indoors.

Kimberly and Kevin always hung around Frank for the support he gave them. They cried a lot away from home. But a few of the kids had started to gravitate toward Courtney that day. Perhaps they recognized one of their own—Courtney could be very kidlike.

During out-of-the-pool time, she sat on a hot-pink towel that said BEVERLY HILLS and had a gold star on it. The lifeguard, who was a real hunk, was staring at her. Well, only with one eye—the other eye was on the pool. But Courtney didn't care. She had sworn off boys to devote her whole life to her acting career. Either that or she didn't find him ABSOLUTELY GOR-

GEOUS. But I swear if that lifeguard had seen that Courtney was there alone or just with me, I bet he would have found some way of getting her phone number. It was just so easy for Courtney to get boyfriends.

"Okay, guys," Frank said at lunchtime. "Let's head off Washington Square Park."

There were some audible boos because they knew they had to walk. They knew the route already.

We got all the kids cartons of chocolate milk for a special treat and bottles of juice for ourselves, and we ate our melty cheese sandwiches in the park. Then after playing a few games, we headed back to the subway with twenty-four sleepy, grumpy, smiley, dopey kids.

It was about five to four when Zora opened the door and said, "Greetings. Sixteen pages. I broke a record. Oatmeal-raisin cookies for one and all as we celebrate my literary muse and the passage of time that has delivered me of fresh prose."

"She's getting worse," Courtney whispered in my ear. "At least before we could understand her most of the time."

I kicked her ever so slightly in the shin. Jobs, even mainly volunteer ones, are hard to come by in New York City, especially when you are only thirteen. That's all I had to do was lose my job. Then for sure I'd be trailing my crazy cousin Courtney all over town on her days off with the police not far behind.

See, I guess, in my unconscious mind I really didn't trust the new not crazy Courtney for a moment. I wanted to believe in her. I really did, but it was hard.

But Courtney had changed, I constantly reassured myself.

Parents were coming to pick up their kids. There was one man, a father who was a freelance artist and did all the household chores. There were also a lot of baby-sitters, and a few mothers who worked part-time.

The next day was Saturday and we'd be off. Also Courtney wasn't called on the set until Monday. We had the whole weekend together.

Suddenly, though, I panicked.

What could we do?

Courtney solved it for me. "Hey, let's go shopping on the way home. There's something I want to buy and there's a store near us that probably has one."

"Do you have any money?" I asked her.

She reached down and pulled out a credit card from her red sock. We were both still wearing our camp uniforms. "And I just got my first paycheck." Then I remembered Courtney had her own credit card.

"But don't you want to put your money in the bank?"

"Nope."

"And I can't talk you into saving it for college?"

39

"Nope."

We walked into a large store and Courtney didn't wait to be waited on. She just walked right up to the salesperson and said, "I'd like to look at one of those."

I embarrassed myself by gasping.

It was a camera. Not an Instamatic camera, not a camera camera. It was a video camera.

"This is our Memorex model one fifty-eight," the salesperson was saying as if Courtney were over five feet. "And, of course, it has an eight millimeter zoom." *Of course.* I didn't like the feel of this. It also occurred to me that I had forgotten to tell Courtney my experience with the Mystery Woman. Courtney could really mix me up.

"And also," the salesperson was chirping, "we have an extra light battery for eighty-nine ninety-nine."

"Well, that's reasonable," Courtney was saying in her Beverly Hills voice. "How much is the camera?"

"It's on sale. Only seven hundred and ninety-nine dollars and ninety-nine cents."

I gasped, choked, sputtered, and otherwise embarrassed myself again.

Courtney smiled and handed her credit card to the salesperson, "Okay, wrap it up."

"With or without the battery?"

"With."

I just knew it would take the salesperson more

than a few minutes for her to check out the card. Courtney was just a kid, after all.

"Courtney," I said, my voice quivering, "do you know what you just did?"

"Yep. See, I have plans, Cath. I can't only be a movie star. People treat movie stars like bimbos, and I need to show the world who I am."

I shook my head. If only they knew.

Now I was perched on the edge. All my senses on red alert. Trouble was bound to happen soon. I never knew exactly when. The salesperson came back, beaming, and handed Courtney her new toy. Meanwhile, I never got a chance to talk to Courtney about the lady on the train because the only thing on her mind and out of her mouth was her new video camera. And Courtney had a one-track mind.

CHAPTER FIVE

Saturday morning Courtney threw together her favorite breakfast—and now mine—Oreo cookies slathered with chunky peanut butter.

"Where to, Cath?" she asked, fondling her new video camera. I could see she was itching to use it.

"Well, let's see, there's the Central Park Zoo and—"

"Okay, first stop the zoo," she said quickly.

We walked all the way through the park to the zoo. By the time we got there, Courtney had built up an appetite and was famished. There were two vendors near the entrance to the park. She bought two hot dogs with mustard and sauerkraut, a bag of chips, and a drink at one. Then she bought an ice cream from the other. All I felt like was a hot dog and some orange juice.

"Are you on a diet or something?" she asked me.

Courtney would never have to diet. She was like a machine who could eat anything she wanted and never show it.

As we walked toward the entrance, Courtney filmed trees and clusters of people.

"Courtney," I explained. "You're wasting your tape. Wait until we get inside."

But Courtney stubbornly shook her head. "No, I can tape over it. See, I'm making a documentary. I have it all planned. It's called *The Central Park Zoo and You.* Maybe I'll win an award or something."

My crazy cousin Courtney hadn't changed her thought processes at all. Basically she saw things one way and the world saw them another.

I didn't want to burst her bubble.

At least not all at once.

"Well, it's not exactly like this is a huge zoo. If you want to see giraffes or bears or gorillas, we'll have to go to the Bronx Zoo or my mother's office."

Courtney was using her zoom lens right then to focus on a rather large, interesting piece of foliage.

I wondered how much more she had charged on her credit card. She was the only thirteen-year-old I bet who had one, even though it was probably in her father's name.

Playing tour guide, I announced, after we paid to get in, "Straight ahead in that big pool with the giant rock are the sea lions. You could wait and film them when they're fed. Then there's the polar bear circle with a lot of cute penguins and a couple of polar bears outside. I love the polar bears. Then there's the tropic zone where you walk around and—"

"Don't forget the thousands of leaf-cutter ants," a woman eavesdropper said.

I nodded and thanked her. Courtney just grinned.

"What do you want to do first?" I asked her. This was the first time Courtney had been fully unleashed on the City of New York since she had arrived, and I developed a fearsome premonition that maybe this wouldn't be a lovely stroll in the park after all.

Courtney had one eye shut, filming anonymous subjects from the bench where she had plopped down.

"Look," I said, helping her decide what to do. "We could go up close to the sea lions and you could wait until one whooshes up and, blam, we get him on film."

"Ummmm," she said.

"We could film the red pandas."

"Ummmm."

"We could go—"

"Shhh. I'm filming."

Suddenly Courtney jabbed me with her elbow. "Don't turn around," she said in a whisper, "but the lady sitting a few feet down from you looks like a vampire."

44

I immediately turned around.

She did.

She was wearing all black, had black hair and bright red lipstick, and her teeth were weird and pointy. She had a rather large overbite. But this was silly—I didn't believe in vampires. I didn't even follow my horoscope.

"Courtney, she's not. This is New York. Everyone's different looking in New York."

"Cathy," she whispered urgently, "I read this book—"

"You read a book?" I interrupted her.

"Well, it was a comic book, but it was about this lady vampire and no one knew she was one, and she tried to hide it, but one day the urge overcame her and she had to have blood so she killed little, defenseless animals."

"And you think that's this woman here?" I said, trembling. Courtney could always do this to me.

Courtney nodded. "She's hungry."

"Oh, my God," I said.

"Now, Cathy, I'm going to pretend to shoot the sea lion or a tree or a bush or whatever, but I'm going to get a close-up of this woman. This is a real story."

I couldn't believe this. No one would believe this. Besides, I remembered somewhere you couldn't photograph vampires or ghosts or witches. They wouldn't show up on the film.

Still, there was no stopping my crazy cousin Courtney, who was humming to herself and busily filming the lady who did look awfully much like a vampire.

Suddenly a man jumped up and grabbed Courtney's camera. He was the man sitting on the other side of the vampire look-alike.

"No pictures!" he shouted. "I don't want no pictures taken of me."

Courtney and I exchanged shocked glances.

He must have thought she was videotaping him. But she was videotaping the woman he was sitting next to, who must be with him. I hadn't even noticed him, but I did guess that his face would be in all the shots.

Or part of his face.

Courtney snatched her camera back.

He reached for the camera again, but Courtney yanked it back in time. "No pictures!"

"He must be a famous singer or some kind of celebrity," Courtney said.

I looked at the vampire woman. She shrugged. "My name is Violet" was all she said.

The man made a desperate snatch at the camera again, and this time he got it and took off running with it up the walk to the entrance. Courtney was fast on his heels shouting, "Stop, thief! Stop, thief!"

I left the vampire woman, who was taking off her black high heels to start after Courtney. She sure could run fast. Then I thought of a subject Courtney said she was definitely good at in school. Gym.

People along the way stopped to watch us.

"Stop, thief!" Courtney and I were yelling.

But the man kept running with Courtney's camera.

Finally we got to the information booth at the entrance to the park, and a man intercepted all three of us.

"Slow down," he said.

"Who are you?" the man with Courtney's camera asked.

"Security. Now, what's going on here?"

The man who had taken Courtney's camera immediately tossed it to the security man as if it were a hot potato.

"She tried to steal my camera. I'm running away from her. She's dangerous."

Courtney and I had our mouths hanging open. This man was crazy. That just wasn't true.

"I'll handle this, Cath," Courtney said. "The fact is, Officer, he stole my camera, and then I stole it back, and then he stole it and took off with it."

I nodded.

The woman who strongly resembled a vampire had caught up with us, her shoes in her hand. "Hi, I'm Amber," she said.

The man from security was more than a little confused.

I could see there was a crowd gathering around us.

We were in the spotlight again.

It was just a matter of hours before we got into serious trouble. I could smell it.

47

"Well, okay. It's her camera," he admitted. "She can have it back as long as she promises not to use it any more. I don't want no pictures!"

"It's a free country!" someone yelled.

A large crowd had gathered, and an old woman had shouted out. Everyone in the crowd agreed with her.

Suddenly the man at the information booth picked up a cellular phone.

"Right. Okay. Gotcha. No one's going anywhere. Ten-four."

It seemed even when we didn't do anything wrong, everything turned out wrong, anyway.

It turned out that the phone call was to the Central Park police, who would be there momentarily.

In no time at all a female officer and a male officer walked up to us, pushing through the crowd.

Courtney was now holding her camera up as if it were a trophy.

The vampire lady smiled, and I could see again how irregular her teeth were. Maybe she liked looking like a vampire.

"My name is Dulcy," she said, changing her name once again.

The man just scowled and stared down at the ground.

"Okay, what's the trouble here?" the female officer asked.

"I'll handle this. This man stole my camera," Courtney said.

At the same time the man said, "She stole my camera."

He had just admitted it was Courtney's, but now he was starting this again.

"Well, whose camera is it?" the male officer said.

"Mine," they both answered together.

"Wait a second, Courtney, I'll handle this," I said. "It belongs to my cousin Courtney, and she has a sales receipt to prove it."

Courtney nodded. "I'm Courtney Green, no *e* at the end, from Beverly, like the girl's name, Hills, California."

Just then the female officer said to the thief, who had the bushiest eyebrows I'd ever seen, "Wait a second. Can I see your driver's license?"

The man took out his wallet and five licenses fell out.

"Wait a second, wait a second," the female officer said as her counterpart picked up the licenses. "I know who this is. Don't you know who this is?"

Her partner shook his head.

"This is Booboo."

There was an audible cry from the crowd. Then people started to ask, "Who's Booboo?"

I turned to Courtney, who was now filming everything.

"I think we're on to something big," she said.

CHAPTER SIX

This is none other than Nick E. "Booboo" Mozzarella, the two-bit con artist," the female officer said.

There was a murmur in the crowd.

"Never heard of him," a couple of people said.

Courtney was still covering the event with her camera.

"He sold toasters that didn't pop up at a street fair," she said.

There was a big boo from the crowd.

"He sold turkey franks to a chain of hot dog stands that expected one hundred percent beef franks," she continued.

"Yuck!" someone from the crowd yelled out.

"Actually turkey franks are better for you," someone else said. "There's less fat."

Courtney spun around to take in the crowd reaction.

"We're going to be famous, Cathy," she said jubilantly.

"Courtney, you're already going to be famous."

"He also supplies those defective portable radios they sell on street corners. Most of them don't last more than a week," the female officer said.

I stole a look at Nick E. Mozzarella. His eyes were cast down, but it looked as if he was looking up.

"I bought one of those radios," a man yelled. "I'm from Scranton, Pennsylvania. Hey, I want my money back!"

Just then Violet/Amber/Dulcy spoke. "Booboo, you got caught," she said sadly.

"Who are you?" the female officer said, spinning around.

She thought for a moment and then said, "Lily."

"Well, we'll have to take you in when we book him. Plus we'll need you little girls to file a report."

Here it comes, I thought. We weren't exactly in trouble but we were in trouble. I didn't know where to draw the line anymore.

The officers were joined by more officers. This wasn't Booboo's lucky day, thanks to Courtney.

"Let's take him to the Central Park precinct and book him there," one officer said.

"Wait a second, is this the north or the south side of the street because if it's in the south side he would go somewhere else."

"It's the north."

They had gone into a huddle. "Listen, this is Detective Yossarian's man. He's been dogging this character for years. Let's take him to the Two-Oh. He'll end up there anyway. Then Yossarian owes us one."

Oh, no, I thought. Not the Two-Oh.

Courtney was getting a shot of all the officers and swinging back to the vampire woman, whom I think she still believed was a real vampire. Courtney could be stubborn that way.

The Two-Oh, or twentieth precinct, was where we had gone when we had gotten into trouble last summer. This was terrible. Yossarian knew us, too.

"Gosh, maybe he'll get five thousand hours of community service and that'll help him," Courtney said.

"That's awful what he did to all those people," I said, clucking my tongue, shaking my head.

Courtney shrugged. "He had a bad beginning, Cath. That's what happens. But turkey franks, they should throw the book at him for that."

We all walked up the road to the entrance with Courtney filming Nick E.'s back. In a squad car Nick E. sat in the front with a hankie over his head, muttering over and over, "No pictures. I said no pictures." Tulip, she had decided to change her name once again, sat in the backseat with Courtney and me. Courtney was busy filming the dashboard of the car.

The twentieth precinct or Two-Oh was between Amsterdam and Columbus Avenue on Eighty-second Street. Courtney filmed a little of the precinct as we waited to go upstairs to the detective bureau.

"Isn't this great, Cath? I've got everything on video. They can call it *Movie Star Shoots Thief.*"

"Courtney, if this gets on national television (and knowing my crazy cousin Courtney it would), they won't give you credit. They'll just have the word *amateur* floating somewhere across the screen." Then I added, "Sorry."

This was hard for me to say, but I knew it was true. So better to hear it now than to have her read it.

Just then a pretty female officer stopped by and put her hand on my shoulder.

"Hi, honey, haven't we met before?"

"At the softball game between the Girl Scouts and Boy Scouts two years ago when the girls baked the cookies and won the game?"

She shook her head.

"No, I was thinking of something more recent. Last summer. I know, you got into trouble with a fake murder. That's it—right?"

53

I wanted to carve a hole through the floor and sink into it. Courtney was shooting the female officer.

Finally someone said to her, "No video cameras in here." Courtney put it down. "And no gum chewing." Courtney slapped it on her wrist. "Unless you have some for the whole precinct."

Everybody laughed.

They had taken "Booboo" Mozzarella upstairs to book him. His accomplice or girlfriend went with him. I wondered if she ever used the same name twice.

Then it was our turn to go up to the detective bureau to talk to Detective Yossarian. He was typing up a report with two fingers on his computer when we came in.

He looked up.

"Haven't I seen you two girls here before?"

"At the picnic when the girls played the boys and the girls baked cookies and won," I said hopefully.

"No," he said, scratching his head. "Now I remember. Last summer. The time when you were involved with the fake murder case." He smiled at us. "Sit down."

Then Detective Yossarian excused himself and left the room for a minute. There was a lady crying in the corner. She wore a coat and a big straw hat with a cluster of plastic cherries on it.

"Hey, would you like to see a tape of a true

crime?" Courtney asked. "It's how I single-handedly captured Nick E. Dooboo Mozzarella.

The woman kept on sobbing.

"It might cheer you up," Courtney said. She was always very warm-hearted.

Detective Yossarian had returned. He wore a tie and a short-sleeved shirt like the detectives on TV.

"Now, you girls tell me what happened."

"Well," Courtney began. "I was filming a documentary in the park."

"Are you a filmmaker?"

"No, I'm a movie star."

"I see," he said.

"Then I saw this woman who was a vampire, although my cousin Cathy doesn't believe in vampires."

I could feel my face turning blush pink. Courtney talked so freely. Sometimes she talked to strangers on the street, too. Courtney just loved people.

"And then this criminal, this 'Booboo' person snatched my camera and ran away with it yelling— 'no pictures!' "

The woman in the corner began to cry louder.

Detective Yossarian was typing up everything we said slowly, with two fingers. Finally he said, "I like this. But I like you two girls even more. I've been trailing Booboo for years, but, just between you and me, I've made a lot of booboos."

Then he sent us downstairs to wait until we were

called upstairs again. But we had only a few minutes to wait before that old familiar crowd came crashing frantically through the door. I had made one call to my mom—and a parade had assembled from it. My mom, who had lost an earring, was followed by Zora Zimmerman in a blue and yellow caftan followed by Howard, whose shoulders were shaking as if there had been an earthquake, a sign he was trying to hold in a laugh, followed by Frank and Mrs. Phillips. At that point I fantasized that the floor of the twentieth precinct would part and let me slip through invisibly.

"My baby," my mom said, rushing up to hug me. She had a beautiful, lush, multicolored parrot perched on her shoulder.

"Mom," I said. "You're bringing your work home with you again."

She tended to be a workaholic.

"This is Eggbert," she said. "He's going to be used for a Club Med commercial, and I'm getting him ready for the shoot."

"Get off my back!" Eggbert squawked.

All the officers and detectives were gawking at this human—and not-so-human—menagerie as they walked by. I just wanted to die of embarrassment. We were the center of attention. We were the center of everything. It was a three-ring circus that was spilling into the precinct room. How long would it be before the reporters and camerapeople trouped in and made the twentieth famous again?

I didn't want to be a heroine.

I wanted to go home and have an icy soda and turn on the TV without seeing myself on it.

Now I knew how Frank felt.

I had had it with today.

But, of course, I would never have my wish. Clint Carothers, Courtney's director, and his publicist, Jerry, rushed in through the door. How had they heard? Then I noticed the grin on Courtney's face and her quick attempt to squelch it. Jerry was chomping on a fat cigar, which was unlit, and talking out of the side of his mouth. "Didn't I tell you, CC?" he said. "This kid is a gold mine of publicity." Tiffany (Courtney) Alicia Green smiled sweetly as the reporters walked on cue, through the door.

Of course, it was obvious who had tipped them off—Jerry.

One of the female officers asked if they should get a cake.

Zora Zimmerman had brought, for a special treat, tuna fish salad sandwiches and oatmeal raisin cookies. Another female officer was taking one of Mrs. Phillips's business cards because she had studied acting in college and always wanted to do television commercials.

Everyone was calling us heroines. Some heroines. All Courtney wanted to do with her $799.99 video camera was shoot a vampire. We had done it again!

57

Eggbert squawked, "You look like a million bucks, kid!"

Maybe it was my fault. Maybe if I could have persuaded Courtney not to get the camera and put her money in the bank, or to shoot the sea lion or not to ogle vampires. Well, there were a million things I *could* have done. But I wouldn't ever want to replace the sheer happiness on Courtney's face.

Courtney was actually trying to sell her tape to the media. She was still my crazy cousin Courtney.

"God save the Queen!" Eggbert squawked, and I realized then that he must be a British parrot. But I wondered if we could pull him out of there before he got a little salty and started swearing. It was as if he had swallowed a tape recorder which rolled on continuously.

But everyone ignored him. He was just like background music in an already noisy situation. Camerapeople were clicking away as the reporters interviewed Courtney, who had reddened her lips by biting them.

Jerry announced that Courtney was filming *The Laundry Bag Murder* but was also a camp counselor at Camp Acorn in the wilderness of Manhattan. Zora Zimmerman handed one reporter a tuna fish salad sandwich and made sure he got the quote and spelled the name of her camp right. Then she told him about her new book, *Be Still My Heart*.

I glanced over at Howard, who was pounding the

wall with his fists. He had given in to a laughing fit. Howard always thought we were so funny.

I wasn't amused.

I was embarrassed.

I wanted it to be over.

I wanted to be home.

I stole a look at Frank, who gave me an encouraging smile. He seemed to know what I was thinking.

Frank and I were alike, I decided.

CHAPTER SEVEN

"Let's get a shot of the two cousins together," one of the photographers said.

"I'm Courtney Green, no *e* at the end, from Beverly, like the girl's name, Hills, California. My stage name is Tiffany," Courtney announced, enjoying it all. Jerry, the publicist, and Clint Carothers beamed back at her, enjoying it more.

I felt miserable.

And naive.

We weren't supposed to get into trouble *this* summer. Courtney was a movie star and I supposedly had a boyfriend. Though I wondered for how long.

Frank was standing quietly in the corner studying the floor.

Howard was slumped against the wall still laughing so hard he was crying.

Everyone wanted to hold Eggbert. And talk to him.

Jerry, the publicist, was talking to the cops about the movie Courtney was making. It was, after all, a detective picture. Courtney and Frank and I had discovered a murderer last summer who wasn't really a murderer, but Courtney had been seen by Clint and got to be a movie star out of it. I just became tremendously embarrassed by all the attention. Frank was also camera shy. It looked as if he was trying to make himself invisible and fade into the institutionally colored wall. I knew the twentieth precinct had never seen anything exactly like my crazy cousin Courtney. They would have a hard time going back to the dullness of arresting criminals and processing Nick E. Mozzarella.

Courtney had truly dazzled them all.

Finally the long ordeal was over and Howard offered to take us all out for ice cream. Why not? There was always a party whenever Courtney forced us into the spotlight.

We all got into cabs with Eggbert singing the British national anthem, or at least that's what I think it was. When we got to an ice cream and frozen yogurt shop the owner refused to let Eggbert in. This got my mom very angry, and she threatened to sue him. Nowhere on the door did it say NO PARROTS ALLOWED. My mom hated discrimination of any kind. Especially of animals. So we bought cartons of ice cream at a store—all of Courtney's favorite flavors—and took them up to our apartment. Besides, it was time for the news. Would we get on it or not? That was the question. Courtney Tiffany Alicia Green had done it again. Created an event.

"See, Cathy," she said to me, scooping the pecans out of her butter pecan ice cream, her major favorite flavor, and feeding them to Wilheim Von Dog, "I told you everything would turn out all right."

I thought for a moment. Actually she hadn't said that at all. What she had said was—that woman is a vampire. That's how it had all started. As Zora would say in one of her romance stories, "my eyes glazed over" as I tried to picture Courtney in the year 2005, when we were all grown up. Where was she heading? What would she be like then?

I was feeling guilty, thinking of all the ways I could have stopped Courtney before our outing turned into an incident.

We turned on the five o'clock news. Only Courtney looked radiant and energetic as we sat down to watch. Everyone else appeared a little wilted around the edges. Eggbert had finally shut up and was in his cage with the cover over it. Wilheim Von Dog lay still like the little fluffball he was. The story on us is going to be on now, I thought. I was developing a sixth sense for press coverage.

I shut my eyes, but I couldn't shut out the announcer's amused voice as he relayed our tale. Two little girl counselors from a day camp apprehended Nick E. "Booboo" Mozzarella. Then they aired the video Courtney had given the reporters. It showed the crowd, Nick E. with a handkerchief over his head, and his vampire accomplice of the five hundred names.

All of the tape was captioned "amateur."

I put my arm around Courtney. I knew how disappointed she was. Now she would have to stick to being a movie star, which most girls of thirteen would have given their eyeteeth for.

Courtney felt a little gypped, I could tell. She had built a career around these stunts and wanted credit for her tape.

When everyone got up to go, my mom said to Courtney and me, "Girls, that's enough excitement for one day." I nodded. Courtney didn't.

Monday morning *Relief* was my middle name as I said goodbye to Courtney, who went back to work on the movie. Sunday had been amazingly quiet. As I walked to Camp Acorn, I looked forward to a normal day of having Frank all to myself and pretending someone dangerous was following me. Of course, all that the little kids wanted to talk about was Nick E. Mozzarella. Their parents must have told them about him.

Zora told them all that good had triumphed over evil and Courtney and I had captured the bad man. I don't think anyone really understood her. Zora talked like she wrote. And this wasn't even a love story.

Then we all lined up to pick up our lunch bags and subway tokens.

"I don't like Swiss cheese anymore," one of the little kids whined.

Half the room agreed with him.

"Yeah," another said. "Let's have Twinkie sandwiches."

I smiled. Things were back to normal, and I could concentrate on Frank.

We took the kids to Central Park, and Frank was the pitcher as we played a few games of softball. It was a perfect summer day. Just what we needed to erase Saturday, when everything had been larger than life. Walking home, Frank held my hand and I felt all tingly inside. Also it was getting easier and easier to talk to him. After all, he had been my friend first.

"I wanted to tell you I liked you the first time I saw you when we were in Beverly Hills, but I just clammed up," Frank admitted. I didn't know boys clammed up that way. "Do girls clam up?" I didn't know what to say—I had clammed up.

"Yeah," I finally got out. I left out—all except for Courtney. The sidewalks on the Upper West Side glistened in the sparkling sunshine. The trash cans were large friendly objects a painter could put in a painting. Everyone seemed to be smiling at us. Frank's hand was in mine. I had my first boyfriend, and he was the greatest guy in the world.

For some inexplicible reason I turned around.

There she was again.

The Mystery Woman for the second time. She was wearing her big white straw hat and the large, round white-framed sunglasses. When I turned all the way around to confront her, she ducked into a doorway. I couldn't believe it. Frank saw her, too. Holy Moley! I had completely forgotten to tell Courtney I had seen the woman on the subway.

"Don't get uptight, Cathy," he said, squeezing my hand. "I'm here."

Boy, had I underestimated my crazy cousin Courtney.

She must have taken some of her hard-earned money, which she was supposed to send to Bernie, and hired an actress to follow me to make it look authentic for Frank.

But still the whole idea of being followed gave me the creeps.

I had never been followed that way.

65

Actually, I had never been followed any way.

She was the same one as on the subway. I let Frank take charge then because he read detective novels and was a big fan of Raymond Petz, the famous mystery writer.

"Cathy," he said when we reached my apartment building, "you go upstairs and I'll try to follow the person who's been following you. See what I can learn."

I wanted to say—Stop! It's just a trick; it's a lie (well, actually it wasn't a lie lie, it was more like a little white lie). Also I had figured out in my mind that if the average person walked down the average crowded street, they would be followed because there were so many people on the street. So everyone was being followed. Actually that seemed pretty feeble, but how could I ever tell him my crazy cousin Courtney had probably hired an actress to follow me to make it appear that I was in danger? That was the trouble with lying. It was really like an avalanche and I was already in a snowdrift up to my shoulders.

When I got up to my apartment, I was surprised to find Courtney sitting cross-legged on the floor braiding little yellow ribbons into Wilheim Von Dog's fur. She was wearing a yellow T-shirt that read "Let Me Entertain You."

"Did you tell him someone was following you?"

I nodded miserably. Courtney and I hadn't really had a chance to talk. We had been too busy at the twentieth precinct, and then on Sunday we had had family time with my mom and Howard.

"Next time, Cathy, you have to tell him you're not sure you like him." She turned Wilheim Von Dog around to do his other side.

"But I do."

"*I* know you do, but it throws guys off their guard, makes them try harder."

I thought of Frank right then searching the streets for the woman who was following me who had been hired by Courtney to make it look like I was being followed and in trouble. Instead he could have been home having a frosty glass of soda, relaxing in his favorite chair in front of the TV.

"Courtney I don't think Frank would like that," I said softly. Even though I knew she was an expert when it came to boys.

A large bubble popped and broke all over Courtney's face.

"Oh, by the way, thank you for having that woman follow me. She's been doing a great job. Frank saw her today, too. How much did it cost you? Maybe I can save up from my allowance to pay you back."

Courtney stared at me, her seaweed green, sky blue eyes clouding over.

"But, Cathy, I didn't pay anyone to follow you," she said innocently.

Too innocently, I decided.

See, I never knew when to believe Courtney (Tiffany) Alicia Green. She *was* a good actress.

I didn't know whether to believe her now or not. But if I didn't, well, who was following ... me?

CHAPTER EIGHT

I had to give my cousin Courtney credit for one thing. She was a hard worker. She got up at five-thirty every morning without having to be coaxed out of bed. She spent five minutes in a cuddling-Wilheim-Von-Dog session and threw together her favorite breakfast. Three fresh Oreo cookies slathered with a mound of chunky peanut butter.

Everything was going smoothly between Frank and me. I understood better how people could be friends and also like each other. I finally decided I didn't believe Courtney hadn't hired that woman to follow me. She must have. So my telling Frank a lie wasn't a lie anymore. Not a real lie anyway. Courtney had really done a superb job. The Mystery Woman had new disguises now. Mostly she wore oversize sunglasses, but in different colors. Sometimes she wore a reddish wig with bangs. Sometimes she wore the wig with a big, floppy white straw hat and a black band. had was beginning to get used to her and I even named her. Tara, she became in my mind. She was a gift, that's all. Courtney loved to give surprise gifts.

"Are you guys going to get married?" one of the little kids asked at Zora's one day. I guess our relationship wasn't a secret. After we got out of Camp Acorn and walked two blocks, we would hold hands and talk.

I turned a rosy red and Frank winked. "Not until next summer," he said. Zora Zimmerman gave me a meaningful glance and smiled. It was just so romantic. She had already confided that the star-crossed lovers in her next book would be named after us. I had read her first book. The lovers in it were kept apart for 465 pages and then finally got together. She really knew how to keep the pages turning. Whenever I had time, I was doing my own writing in my little purple notebook.

Everything was terrific until one afternoon when Courtney made an announcement that hit like a thunderbolt. I had been totally unprepared for it. She was sitting with Wilheim Von Dog, who had on a big plaid bow. She was wearing a matching plaid top and jeans.

"What are you doing home so early?" I asked.

Even as I said it I had those funny butterflies in my stomach. They were the trumpets that sounded before a major announcement.

"I'm through," she said dramatically, flinging her arms high into the air.

I plopped down on the sofa. "Courtney, they didn't fire you, did they?" Maybe it was her criminal record.

She laughed. "No, Cathy, my part in the movie is finished. I'm free to work at Camp Acorn. I can hang out with you and Frank."

I wanted to rush to call Mrs. Phillips to see if she could get Courtney another job. Fast. I couldn't have Courtney unleashed on New York and me. Not just yet. Not when I was having such a lovely time with my first-time-ever boyfriend.

"How's everything in the Frank department?" she asked, blowing a bubble. Before I had a chance to answer that he wasn't a department, he was a boy, she reminded me I had to feed Chino. Chino was the baby leopard my mom was baby-sitting. He was going to shoot a commercial for fake fur coats. The concept was to be against wearing real fur. Chino was kind of spoiled. He would only sleep in the bathtub. My mom threw in a couple of plants to keep him happy. It looked like an offbeat jungle scene. But Chino was civilized, too. At least as much as a wild animal can be. He had a sweet tooth. His trainer

71

had always rewarded him with marshmallows when he did something well. My mom decided to keep feeding him marshmallows, so he didn't get depressed.

My mom and her assistant, Scottie, the fastest typist in all of New York, were very much into animal psychology.

Courtney was now chain-chewing bubble gum. She would chew a piece, get the flavor out, slap it on her hand nervously, wrap it up, and put another piece in her mouth. Zora didn't allow gum chewing at Camp Acorn, so Courtney was having one last binge before withdrawal.

"Life will be so dull," Courtney was moaning in her movie star voice, which was a perfect imitation of some old movie star I had seen in a movie once.

"I shall just be existing," she said dramatically.

"Courtney," I said, knowing she'd have this letdown. "Your father, I mean Bernie, made you a deal. You could do the movie if you went back to Camp Acorn." (Well, I really meant back down to earth.) "We can go to museums, parks, movies, zoos—well, on second thought, we'd better not go to zoos."

We were both quiet. I could sense her wheels spinning. Camp Acorn wouldn't be enough for her. She would want to get us into trouble again.

Finally it hit me.

The one thing Courtney would be interested in.

"Courtney, what about a boyfriend?" I said.

Suddenly she was the old Courtney again. "Wow! Super! That would be fantastic, Cathy. So who do you know?"

"Nobody."

"Well, how do girls meet guys in New York?"

"How do they meet guys in Beverly Hills?"

"They just meet them."

She nodded knowledgeably. Courtney had never had a problem meeting boys. Well, that was an understatement. But producing an instant boyfriend like buying a box of detergent in the supermarket— well, that would be different.

That reminded me that I had to pick up some things for my mom at the supermarket. Courtney and I walked over, and at the entrance to the door Courtney found some free community newspapers. As I was getting my cart, I heard her shriek. I looked at the cover page: CITY PLANNERS TALK ABOUT REZONING UPPER WEST SIDE. I didn't know Courtney was interested in municipal politics.

"Look at this, Cathy," Courtney said, pointing her finger at the paper. "The personal ads." She flipped immediately to the columns. There went my familiar butterflies. We were about to do it again—go on another Courtney adventure. I only knew one thing. It was useless for me to stop them. However, this seemed relatively harmless. Who would answer her ad? She was just a kid.

Courtney picked up the newspapers and folded

them under her arm while I bought two large chuck steaks, three bags of marshmallows, and a box of cereal for us.

On the way home Courtney started to recite some of the ads to me.

"Look, Cathy. 'Sailor Seeks Romance. Share the tiller with me. Set a course of adventure with my heart. I delight in choppy waves.' "

I thought to myself, There would be no problem with Courtney aboard.

" 'I seek a mate who is more than a fair-weather friend,' " she read. " 'I've explored the Amazons and would like to explore you. Note/photo necessary.' "

"How old is he?" I asked.

"It doesn't say," Courtney said. "He must be young. He probably just got out of the navy. Maybe he joined early and now he's eighteen," Courtney said delightedly.

"Or sixty," I muttered under my breath.

"Here's another one," she said, almost bumping into someone. I was trying to remember if Chino took his steak rare with ketchup or medium rare with Worcestershire sauce. But I figured he would be more interested in the marshmallows. It seemed my mom specialized in eccentric clients, but not one of them could surpass my cousin Courtney in eccentricities.

" 'Producer Seeking Leading Lady. Six feet, fit, eyes of blue, would like to meet pretty lady with zest for living.' " (Well, that was an understatement with Courtney.) " 'to share my life and be my love. Note/photo.' "

It sounded like a song.

"Courtney, I don't think you should answer those. You, or I mean we, might get into trouble." It was always, ultimately, we anyway.

Courtney didn't seem to hear me. She had a way of doing that. She kept right on talking. "No age here, either, Cath. Poor guy. He's probably like me. Alone and lonely in New York."

"Courtney, you're not alone. Besides, he's too old for you. He's a producer. You don't do that after high school."

"Sometimes in Beverly Hills you do," she said matter-of-factly. "It depends on your connections."

She folded the newspaper back under her arm, smiling contentedly. Courtney had a plan. She always had a plan, and her plans always got us into unplanned trouble. However, I had to admit to myself—personal ads seemed harmless enough. Besides, it wasn't as if they would write her back or anything. She was just a kid.

I did think, though, that Zora Zimmerman should get a look at some of those ads for book ideas.

Giggling, we turned the corner. When we got home I fed Chino, who then took a long nap. (We took him out when we needed showers.) Mom had explained to me that Chino needed a lot of rest before he had to work because he was temperamental. He also needed some time away from his trainer because he was too dependent on him. My mom really knew animals.

Courtney and I went into the bedroom, and I gave her some of my powder blue stationery. Sucking on a pen, she thought for a while.

"Dear Box three-four-two-two," she said out loud.

She was probably old enough to be the producer's daughter and young enough to be the sailor's kid sister. I was relieved that she was engaged in any activity that kept us out of the city's precincts.

"No, maybe it should be 'Dear Fair-weather Friend, I am a romantic by night, movie star by day.' "

Wow, I thought.

" 'You might say I'm a child/woman who knows what I want. My vital statistics are strawberry blond curls and blue-green eyes, depending on where the sun is. I have a slim figure and I'm about five feet two. I'm a homegrown Californian.' "

"Gee, Courtney, I didn't know you could write like that," I said, sitting cross-legged on my twin bed with the pink bedspread.

"Only to boys," she replied.

She signed it, "Mate me." I could see her taking a couple pictures out of her wallet. I handed her an envelope.

Next she wrote to the producer. This was right up her alley, I could tell.

" 'Call me a movie star. Call me an enchantress, call me a child/woman, call me at—Cathy, what's the phone number here? I forgot."

My mouth was open.

Courtney really *could* write. Maybe if, like her acting tricks, she could pretend she was writing to a boyfriend with every term paper or book report, she would get better grades. I thought of my manuscript sitting in my bottom drawer. I still hadn't shown it to her. There hadn't been time—or maybe I was too shy.

She licked the envelope and then reached for Wilheim Von Dog, who was sitting at the bottom of the bed dying to be picked up. My mom thought there was sibling rivalry between him and Chino.

Courtney padded into the kitchen and got a handful of marshmallows, which Wilheim Von Dog studied. Then we took him out for his walk and mailed the two letters I knew were just writing exercises for Courtney. She had conveniently left out her age. But in Courtney fashion—that wouldn't constitute lying.

She had just merely left it out.

CHAPTER NINE

All the little kids loved Courtney. They called her "Courtney, Courtney, movie star." Courtney loved kids, animals, and anyone in trouble, which almost always added up to trouble. But for one whole week Courtney acted almost normal.

In the evening the almost normal Courtney and Frank, who was still holding my hand, and I walked up Broadway for ice cream.

"I think I'll have a scoop of chocolate mint and mango and pistachio," Courtney babbled away. Then, "Oh, my God!

"Courtney, what's wrong?" I asked.

"It's—it's—it's—"

"Courtney, spit it out," I said. But I could see for myself. I knew she didn't have her autograph book.

But I could see for myself.

Almost a block away there was this tall guy with black curly hair walking with five other guys. For a moment I felt a sense of déjà vu. He was someone I knew I knew, but he was in the wrong place.

"Rock!" Courtney screamed.

The tall guy turned. "Courtney!" he yelled.

"Rock!" Courtney shouted, cupping her hands like a megaphone in front of her mouth.

"Courtney!" came the reply.

The problem was there was an ocean of people walking between them and no one could move either way. We were where everyone was standing in line for a movie.

"Rock!" some kid yelled, laughing.

Another kid giggled. "Courtney, oh, Courtney!"

Finally Rock and his five friends and Courtney and Frank and I got together.

"Courtney, blimey, look at you. What are you doing in NYC?"

"Making a movie," Courtney said proudly. "What about you?"

"Oh, me and my mates are playing in a club in the East Village. These are the Dinosaurs." The five guys, a head shorter than Rock and almost look-alikes, said, in unison, "Hi."

Courtney lit up like a Christmas tree. All I could

79

think of was the wasted postage on her personal ad letters. When I visited Courtney in Beverly Hills for Christmas vacation, I met one of her boyfriends, Gavin, an absolute hunk, but about as deep as a buttonhole. That hadn't bothered Courtney. Rock was Gavin's part-time gardener, and he was also a rock singer.

It seemed as if he had made it now.

"I asked about you when you were gone," Courtney said helplessly. I did a double-take. She did? She never said anything about Rock.

"Oh, I went back to England right after Christmas," Rock explained. "But it was right here in NYC where I wanted to be." I noticed then that Rock often spoke as if he were singing songs. "Came right here after the clock struck midnight New Year's Eve, bong, bong, bong. It's a love of a city."

He pronounced *love*—loove.

"Oh, Rock," Courtney was cooing. "I just loove the way you talk. Don't you loove the way he talks?" she asked us, acting like Tiffany the movie star.

"Uh-huh," Frank and I said.

I remember thinking maybe the way *we* talked sounded a little funny to him.

"Why don't you come over to the apartment sometime," Courtney said.

Good thinking, Courtney. It would have taken me a year to blurt that out.

At almost the same time Rock said, "Why don't

you come to the club and watch me perform? Why not this Friday night? There are fewer people there than on Saturday night."

Super. Weird to the max. He had asked Courtney out almost faster than she had asked him in.

Courtney had met her match.

Actually I liked Rock. He was a little like Frank but with a British accent and musically inclined.

Suddenly I was staring up into Frank's amber-flecked brown eyes, and he was looking down into mine. "Would you like to go to the club, Cathy?"

He had actually asked me out on a date.

It would be my first *real* date with a boy.

Rock explained to us that sometimes the club was used for poetry readings or rock concerts. It was in the East Village and was called the Nowhere Club.

Rock gave Courtney the address. On the way home I could see her eyes shining under the light of the full moon, and I knew she liked him. One thing about my crazy cousin Courtney, she didn't have long to wait between boyfriends. She attracted them like flypaper.

"What's up, girls?" my mom asked as Courtney and I raced into the apartment, trying to push through the door together as we often did. My mom was sitting with Wilheim Von Dog at her feet and another client, Cartwright, the baby kangaroo, who was spending the night in the guest room. He was doing a series of commercials for an airline. Little Cartwright was munching on a throw pillow.

"Mom, Mom, I have a date!" I shouted. The Frank department had finally come up with something to talk about.

"And Courtney was asked out by Rock, this guy from Liverpool, England. Well, I mean she knew him in Beverly Hills, and then she saw him on Broadway." Right then I realized we forgot to get ice cream. "He's singing at this coffeehouse where they read poetry in the East Village."

I could see my mom didn't know what to say. We were under age.

Finally she said, "Okay, you can go as long as it's clearly a double date. Because you're still only thirteen years old and the East Village, well, it's not the safest place in the world. My little baby is going out on her first date." I was hoping my mom wouldn't cry. She tended to get very sentimental about things like that.

As we went into the bedroom, Courtney began to instruct me on how to act on a first date.

"Now, Cathy, don't be so straight, play it cool, and remember to listen to *everything* he says. And he's supposed to pay, not you. Don't get suddenly generous. Anyway, you don't have any money."

Suddenly I felt my face turning pink and my ears start to feel like toast.

"Look, Courtney, you do it your way and I'll do

it my way. I've been doing just fine with Frank. He likes me. So I'll keep doing it my way. With the exception of that lady you hired to follow us. She's doing a real good job."

Courtney was just about to say something, but we were interrupted. My mom was yelling in a rather strained voice, "Courtney, dear, could you come out here a minute?"

I trailed Courtney into the living room. Howard was shaking hands with a man. I hadn't even heard the doorbell ring. I only knew that my face was still a pale shade of beet red and I was starting to feel guilty that I had gotten angry at Courtney, who was only trying to be helpful.

"Courtney, your, uh, date is here," my mom said awkwardly. "Could you, uh, follow me to the kitchen?" Courtney and I followed her.

We stared across the room as we left, and this shortish guy with his hair combed from the back to the front, obviously to cover a huge bald spot, and old enough to be Courtney's father, stared back at us and smiled. He was wearing a deep burgundy sport coat and a navy shirt open at the collar revealing graying chest hairs and three gold chains.

When we got into the kitchen, my mom asked patiently, "Now, Courtney, who is this man? And why is he your date?"

Courtney turned on her innocent act. It was hard to be angry with Courtney for anything because she always said in a plaintive voice, "Are you mad at me?" It was also hard to punish her, which might be the reason she never got punished.

"Well, Ph-Phyllis," she said, stumbling, "I don't know exactly who he is, but I did answer some personal ads. It was just that I was so lonely and I didn't have a boyfriend."

Yeah, right, I thought.

My mom put her hands up in a stop sign. "Okay, okay, I don't really understand all this, but the rules are no dating older men."

As we walked back into the living room, Courtney said, "Did you see this guy? He's middle-aged. He looks almost thirty."

"I hope you don't mind my stopping by, Courtney," the personal ad date said as we entered the room. "But you put your address on your letter, and I don't live far from here. I was just going out for some ice cream. Actually, you should never put your address on a personal ad letter. It's not safe. However, I can see you don't live alone." He was looking straight at Cartwright, who was hopping around.

I heard a light snort. It was Howard. My mom had sent him to a doctor for his sinuses. But he only laughed that snorty way when he thought we did something funny. I hoped he wouldn't slide to the floor laughing.

"So, Courtney," he said. "You don't look anything

like your picture. It didn't do you justice. You're a lot younger a whole lot younger."

Howard hiccuped.

I figured it out.

Courtney had sent him a picture of her mother.

"You're the sailor," Courtney said.

"I'm the producer," the man said somewhat indignantly. "I do made-for-television films. Sometimes I do documentaries. My last film was *Jungle Jim.*"

My mom immediately perked up and said, "Would you like to have some coffee or iced tea or maybe some lemonade?"

"I'll have what he's having," he said, joking and pointing to Cartwright, who was hopping on the couch and jumping on the throw pillow.

My mom dashed into the kitchen and brought out a silver tray of frosty glasses of iced tea dotted with lemon slices. She put out two little bowls for the animals to drink. It was really a hot, sticky night.

Everyone sat down.

"New York can be a lonely city," the producer said. "It's hard to meet people."

My mom nodded sympathetically, passing him the Sweet'n Low. Cartwright had hopped up on the producer's lap, and Howard was having trouble holding in his snorts and hiccups.

"Tell me something," the producer, who told us his name was Allan, said to my mom, "are *you* single?"

By this time Howard had disappeared into the kitchen, and we heard a pounding noise. It could only be fists beating on the countertop as he laughed. Courtney explained to Allan, in the best Courtney way, that she was sorry. It was all a mistake.

"See, I was alone in New York and I had just finished this major motion picture I was starring in when I thought, What to do? What to do?"

(She had a job at Camp Acorn, but I noticed she conveniently left that out.)

"So I answered personal ads," she continued, "which I think are so convenient, don't you? Then, as fate would have it, an old beau, well, flame, actually, came back into my life, and I realized my life wasn't truly over—so I'm not available."

Allan stared at her. Finally he said to my mom, "Does she have an agent?"

My mom nodded.

He took out his business card and said, "Have the agent call my office in the morning."

My mom rushed to get one of her business cards with little animals on it.

"If you ever need a really talented giraffe or whatever," she said.

CHAPTER
TEN

On Friday after camp my mom wanted us both to go directly to Phyllis's New Zoo for some Dating Etiquette, as she called it. She was always busy at work, so I could tell this was important to her. As we walked in, Scottie, my mom's assistant, was talking on the phone and typing at the same time. I could see Courtney's eyes light up. It was just such a colorful place. Much more fun than Phyllis's Zoo had been. A chimpanzee was sitting in a corner leafing through a copy of *Time* magazine and smoking a cigar. Two small sleek cougars, the color of gray mink, were sleeping like bookends in cages in the corner. There was also a coffee and juice bar for the trainers.

Courtney let out a low whistle before she tickled the chimpanzee and said, "Kootchy, kootchy, koo."

"Wow, this place has sure been duded up," she said.

There were two telephones in the waiting room in case the trainers had to make calls. A sign declaring PHYLLIS'S NEW ZOO in big, gold block letters looked down at us. I was really proud of my mom. She had made it.

"Oh," Courtney squealed.

She was standing over the wastebasket staring into it. Something hadn't changed. Ginger, the piglet—well, actually this was a new Ginger, the other one had grown up—was resting there in a nest of newspaper. A Ginger was always the office mascot. This one was up for a fat-free bacon commercial.

Scottie pulled Courtney's hands away from the wastebasket rim. "Uh-uh, you'll traumatize her, and she has bad stage fright as it is."

A cage full of parakeets were chirping away, but we could still hear my mom talking from her plush office.

"Sorry, sweetheart, no deal. The job calls for Buster to go to Hawaii. They can't shoot his scenes separately on the Upper West Side. Yes, they'll provide suntan lotion. Well, of course, he'll stay at the finest hotel, that's part of the deal. Doggie biscuits?

They'll be coming out of his little ears. So, what do you say? Have we got a deal?"

Courtney and I listened. My mom always got the deal. She was a terrific negotiator.

Finally we could hear her say on the conference phone, "Send the girls in now."

Courtney and I sat in the two big chairs facing her desk.

"Nice place you have here," Courtney said.

"Now, girls," my mom began. "I'm very busy. But tonight is the big double date." My mom always had a different personality in the office from the one she had at home. "You have a curfew."

I could hear Courtney let out a *whoosh* of breath.

"I want you home at eleven."

"But even Cinderella got to stay out until twelve," Courtney said.

Courtney was a good negotiator, too. She had had plenty of practice in Beverly Hills.

"Eleven o'clock," my mom repeated. I knew this was hard for her. I knew it was made harder by the fact I wasn't her little girl anymore. I was an almost teenager—and I was on my first real date.

I knew why she had given us a curfew. She's the biggest worrywart in the world. She just didn't want to stay up all night and end up a frazzled, crazy nervous wreck.

"Also, I know you are young ladies, but I didn't

89

know whether to let you go alone. At first I was going to have Howard take you—"

"Oh, Mom," I said.

"But you'll be with Frank and he's such a responsible and mature young man. Besides he's from the, uh, Midwest."

She reached into her bag and handed us two twenty-dollar bills. "I want you to take cabs. And here's some quarters if you need to call us. In addition, I want you to return home—together. It's a double date, which means you can take care of each other, or at least Cathy can take care of Courtney. Both young men can see you to the door. They can even come up for a soft drink, as long as they do it before eleven."

This time I heard a loud groan from Courtney, but my mom didn't pay any attention. I could see her mind was on the next deal.

"Believe me, Courtney, this is for your own good. New York can be a dangerous city unless you're careful. This isn't Beverly Hills."

"Where everybody drives," they said together.

"But most of all," she said, ripping a Kleenex out of the box on her desk—my mom could be very sentimental—"most of all, I want you to have fun. These are the most precious years of your life. Just be home by eleven."

Then Scottie yelled, "White Chocolate's trainer on four." Somehow he never missed a beat talking and typing. I knew our time with my mom was over as she blew us kisses. "Jocko, how sweet of you to call. Well, we haven't worked out the terms yet, but it looks real good. You'll be feeling your oats. Top billing." White Chocolate was the star of my mom's agency. He was an all-white horse with a chocolate brown tail. No one was allowed to ride him unless he was in a movie. I thought he was a little spoiled.

Courtney and I slipped out the door careful not to disturb the zoo in the waiting room.

We had exactly one hour and a half to get ready.

It wasn't enough time.

Before we knew it the doorbell rang. Frank was wearing jeans and a shirt with a sport jacket. I still couldn't get over how handsome he was. He was my boyfriend and friend now, but every once in a while I felt a heart-stopping crunch that made me slightly incoherent. I was wearing a lilac top that Courtney insisted I wear, and Courtney had on a blazing orange cotton sweater that made her hair look like sunshine.

Howard smiled and pressed a bill into Frank's hand. "Here's a little something extra for ice cream."

We hailed a cab and Courtney announced, "The Nowhere Club. Avenue D."

But the Nowhere Club turned out to be nowhere. Even the cab driver couldn't find it. We had to get out and walk. It had started to drizzle, and the streets seemed grayer and drearier than they were. I had a feeling the cab driver hadn't been too happy in this neighborhood.

I glanced at the people walking by and saw that they were radically different with their coat collars turned up, shaved heads, earrings dangling from their ears or noses, and cigarettes dangling from their lips.

"Maybe we should ask someone," I said.

But at that moment there was no one walking by to ask. Finally we saw a couple and Courtney went up to them. I shut my eyes, hoping she wouldn't go through her Courtney with an *e* speech, but, thankfully, she didn't.

"Do you know where the Nowhere Club is?"

They laughed. "You're standing right in front of it."

Looking down, we saw the Nowhere Club was in a cellar with a little sign that said, NOWHERE CLUB. It was easy to miss, which we had. When we walked in, I got a major case of butterflies. This wasn't really a place where they only had poetry readings and stuff. It was a bar. There were people standing and sitting, glasses hung upside down from the ceiling, and behind the bar there was a big, muscular bartender. I tapped Courtney on the shoulder.

"Courtney, this is a real live bar where they drink alcohol. Maybe we'll get into trouble. Maybe we should leave." It wasn't as if I had lied to my mom, but I could feel her disapproval all the way downtown.

"Oh, my God," Courtney said.

"I had expected something different," I whispered. "Look, I think we're the youngest ones here."

"Listen, I've been around people who drink a lot. I always order a lemonade. Let's sit down and do that." Then I could see she had spotted Rock, who had spotted her, and she was orbiting around another planet. I tried desperately to remember the Courtney who had declared she was off boys. Rock and the Dinosaurs were onstage—actually, they were good. Rock wrote his own songs. I watched him wink at Courtney when we sat down, and I noticed her big smile back at him. There was no way anyone could get Courtney out of this bar.

A waitress came up to our table to take our orders. She was wearing a black leotard, a black mini dress, and had long, stringy black hair.

"A lemonade," Courtney said.

"The same for me," I said shakily.

"On the rocks," Courtney added.

"I'll have a ginger ale," Frank said.

The waitress seemed to snicker. "Sorry, we're all out of lemonade. As a matter of fact, I don't think we ever had it."

We changed our order to Cokes, and the waitress walked away chuckling to herself.

Then I noticed a waiflike creature wander into the

smoke and dim lighting. He was very delicate and his mouth was set in a half-smile, but he looked as if he might cry. He reminded me of a picture of a clown who might be hanging in a child's room. He was passing out yellow daisies with attached slips of paper that said "Peace, love, joy" on them.

Someone gave him a dollar, but he waved it away. He wasn't a panhandler.

"Isn't that sweet," Courtney said. Courtney was very sentimental.

But I could see, out of the corner of my eye, that he had taken something out of his pocket. He was showing a shiny silver watch to a man at a far table. The man took out a roll of bills and paid him for it.

Avenue D was sure a weird place.

Suddenly the big, burly bartender stepped out and said, "Okay, buddy, that's enough. Take your daisies and go somewhere else." He picked him up bodily and threw him out the door. I guess it was a one-man show. He was the owner, the bartender, and the bouncer. Maybe he had an allergy to flowers.

All through this, Rock and the Dinosaurs acted very professionally—they just kept playing.

But then pandemonium broke loose. A lot of people sitting at the bar began to protest. It was easy to see that some of them were so drunk they didn't know what they were protesting about.

"Unfair!"

"You're violating his rights!"

"Let the daisy person back in!"

"I'll buy him a drink!"

The bartender just stood there with his hands on his hips and said, like a little kid, "Well, it's *my* bar."

Meanwhile, we could see that the situation was getting really heated up. The men sitting at the bar were starting to take sides. I could see out the window that the daisy person was standing in the rain handing out daisies as some of the men went out to drag him back inside.

"Wait a second," a man outside said. "He didn't give me my change."

I shut my eyes. It was happening again. Courtney was smiling at Rock. Rock was playing. Everyone was screaming and shouting. It all happened like dynamite igniting. I was praying it wouldn't get worse. I closed my eyes and began to cry silently. But when I heard my crazy cousin Courtney say, "Super!" I knew my prayers wouldn't be answered.

CHAPTER ELEVEN

The brawl then got into full swing.

A fist-slinging, all-out fight that resembled those in old cowboy movies. Nobody really knew who they were jabbing at, and I got the impression they did that at the Nowhere Club. Maybe it eased the tensions.

The poor, sad-eyed daisy person, who had started the ruckus, was trying to inch back out the door. This must have been his prime-time for selling watches. A couple of strong-armed men pulled him back, convincing him, "Don't worry, buddy, you can stay."

People started to skid all over on wet, crumpled daisies.

"Duck!" Courtney instructed.

There was nowhere to go but under the table, so under it we went. Rock and the Dinosaurs kept playing bravely as kind of background music to the punches and grunts.

I could see out of the corner of my eye that the daisy person had sold another two watches. It had been a good night for him. I was glad because it wasn't such a good night for us. We were in trouble again!

And then I couldn't believe what I saw. I nudged Courtney. Under the table directly across from us I saw a pair of eyes covered by a pair of very large sunglasses.

It was the Mystery Woman in one of her very large hats. She must have followed us. I tapped Courtney on the shoulder, but she was too busy gazing up at Rock to answer me.

I closed my eyes then and prayed as the noise got louder and louder. A man slammed and slid across our table, and then he staggered up and punched someone else.

I fished around in my pocket for the quarter my mom had given me to call her if we got in trouble. It would come in handy at the police precinct. We'd done it again.

Really done it again!

The Nowhere Club wasn't a tacky little coffee-house where they read a little outrageous poetry. It was a sleazy grown-up bar that specialized in brawls. I could feel a trickle running down my back and realized that someone had knocked over my Coke and it was dripping off the table.

Where was Frank? Suddenly I realized he was missing.

Then I saw him. He was fighting with someone. Frank? I could see the sleeve of his sport jacket was ripped.

Then, before I could stop her, my crazy cousin Courtney hopped up on top of our table. I tried to pull her back, but what I saw next truly amazed me—and I thought I had seen everything. But then everything about my crazy cousin Courtney amazed me.

She opened her mouth and stuck her fingers in each side. Then she let out an ear-splitting whistle. The whole place stopped fighting then, thinking there had been a raid. Even Rock and the Dinosaurs stopped playing for a minute, but Rock was laughing, I could tell.

"Okay, now!" Courtney yelled. "Stop all this fighting and turn around and hug your neighbor." I could see the daisy person handing out what he had left of his yellow daisies. I could also see that several people were wearing silver watches.

It worked.

My crazy cousin Courtney had done it again!

Everyone stopped brawling and started to laugh.

I could see that laughter was another natural release for their emotions. I would have to jot that down in my purple writers' notebook later.

"Courtney, where did you learn to whistle like that?" I hissed.

"In camp," she whispered back.

"Well, what's it going to be?" Courtney yelled from our tabletop. "Everyone stop fighting or I keep whistling."

Everyone was laughing. Even the Mystery Woman under her table. I could see her shoulders shaking.

Rock and the Dinosaurs were laughing, too.

Soon the whole place was laughing and hugging, and people were buying drinks for one another.

I couldn't help but marvel at all the things Courtney could do. Mrs. Phillips should put it on her résumé. Pro bubble gum blower. Good with kids. Specializing in antics, and now—whistling with two fingers in her mouth.

At first I heard a little click. I couldn't imagine what it was. But then I knew. It was a camera. I hoped it was someone taking pictures for a scrapbook.

I somehow knew I couldn't be that lucky.

Frank had come back to our table with the guy he had been fighting. He was from Brooklyn but had a lot in common with Frank.

The photographer came up and introduced himself.

"Hi, I'm Flash Reardon. Here's my card."

Courtney and I looked at it. It had a little picture of a camera and said, "Gallery Shows, Weddings, and Bar Mitzvahs."

"Does anyone have a quarter?" he asked. "Business has been a little slow lately, but this could be a real scoop. I'd like to call the papers."

Courtney brightened up, gave him a dazzling smile, and fished out a quarter.

Courtney smiled up at Rock and revealed her best profile, her right side. I knew because I had seen her admire it for hours in front of a mirror.

"Well, I certainly can't stop a gentleman of the press," she said in her phony southern belle accent. "My name is Courtney Green, no *e* at the end, and I'm from Beverly, like the girl's name, Hills, California."

"Uh-oh," we heard like a chorus.

In through the door trouped the men and women in blue. New York's Finest had arrived. I shut my eyes, mumbling an improvisational prayer that maybe it wouldn't be too bad. Maybe they would leave. Maybe they had more important cases down the street or on Avenue C.

"Who started it this time?" an officer said.

"The daisy man," a very inebriated man at the bar said.

"Oh, sure, blame everything on the street people," a man, wearing two daisies in his lapel, said.

Then my crazy cousin Courtney raised her hand. "It was everybody's fault." She was always fair. Everybody nodded. It was.

"Aren't you a little young to be in a place like this at night?" a female police officer asked her.

Everyone laughed.

It wasn't funny—at least not to me. Our curfew was still eleven o'clock, and who knew what was coming next. It didn't take long to find out. Four turquoise and white squad cars from the ninth precinct were parked outside, and we all trooped in, five to a car.

The ninth precinct turned out to be on Fifth Street, a very colorful neighborhood in the East Village. Courtney nudged me in the shoulder pointing out the thrift shops and vintage clothing shops. We went through big, impressive wooden doors and the first thing I saw was—WELCOME TO THE 9TH PRECINCT!—in handwritten letters.

There was also a wooden counter and a complaint room. The precinct was crowded and bustling already, but when we piled in with twenty people, it was packed. The pro-daisy people were trying to stuff themselves into the complaint room. The anti-daisy people were trying to blame the whole thing on them.

I shut my eyes.

101

Another three-ring circus starring my crazy cousin Courtney.

A very handsome police officer had given her his police hat to wear. I have to admit she looked really cute in it.

I felt like my head was spinning. Then I had a sobering thought. Courtney hadn't gotten us into trouble. It was just as much my fault as hers. In fact, it was more my fault, all my fault really, because I had agreed to go. And I should have known better. I lived in New York City.

I looked around for Frank. He was busy talking to the guy from Brooklyn about sports and detective stories. I was glad he had a friend.

It was ten to eleven when it was my turn to use the phone to call my mother, who predictably had hysterics. At eleven-thirty she dashed into the precinct dragging a sputtering Howard and Mrs. Phillips.

She immediately hugged me and then Courtney so that we were almost out of breath. Just at that moment Rock and the Dinosaurs came in because they had closed the bar for the night.

Finally the sergeant in charge waved his hands and said, "You can all go home and get some sleep. The owner is not going to press charges."

I thought about that. Actually the owner had started it.

Then I had a sudden urge to fess up to my mom

about this strange lady that Courtney had following me because I was telling this lie to Frank so he would think I was this helpless girl. Then I thought maybe I'd better not. But I couldn't help but notice the Mystery Woman hadn't come with us to the ninth precinct. She had gotten off scot-free, or maybe they had taken her to another precinct.

Frank took my hand in his. The guy from Brooklyn waved goodbye and promised to call.

"Why don't we go for ice cream?" Howard said, trying to compose himself and then not making it. One of the officers came up to him and said seriously, "Are you okay, sir? I know, I have daughters of my own." Howard had another laughing attack.

Late that night after Courtney had had a combination of pumpkin and peppermint-stick ice cream and said goodbye to Rock and the Dinosaurs, Frank and I lingered downstairs in the shimmering moonlight counting the stars. I had never been much good at finding the Big Dipper and the Little Dipper. I only knew that Frank's warm hand was snug in mine. I felt like the heroine in one of Zora Zimmerman's romance novels.

Then Frank leaned over and I felt his lips brush mine. He cupped my chin with his hands and said, "You're special, Cath, and don't ever forget it." And then he walked away.

I just stared after him. No boy had ever kissed me before.

When I went upstairs I was a little dazed.

But no one saw it—except my mom. She just smiled at me. I must have looked goofy. But it was my private kiss, and I didn't want Courtney yelling "Super!" about it.

Except it was super!

CHAPTER TWELVE

About a week later on a Saturday, Courtney sat moping in the kitchen. My mom and Howard had gone out. There was a baby cheetah curled up asleep on a throw rug in the living room. Her name was Zelda, and she was supposed to appear in a fragrance commercial.

"We're never alone," Courtney moaned. She was sitting with her hands cupped under her chin, sighing, drawing circles with her finger on the tablecloth.

"That's ridiculous, Courtney," I said. "We're kind of alone now."

"Not us," Courtney said. "It's Rock. Whenever he comes over, it's with the Dinosaurs. Wherever we go, the Dinosaurs come with us. If there's one stool at the ice-cream shop, we have to wait until five stools are free. If he holds my hand, they stare at us. Once he kissed me on the front step, and all five Dinosaurs kissed me after that. I just don't know what to do."

Courtney really liked Rock. I could tell. She had changed in the past week. We had stayed out of trouble, too.

Maybe Rock was a good thing. It would be good to keep him around.

Suddenly it hit me.

"Courtney, I've got it!"

"What, what do you have, Cath?"

"Rock is shy."

Who knew the symptoms better than I?

"You mean all the time I thought he was the sophisticated rock star and I—"

"Yes! You're the dazzling movie star! We have to map out a strategy," I explained and then we both exploded with laughter. "Why don't you just tell him to leave his Dinosaurs at home. You like him just the way he is."

"I never thought of being honest."

"Courtney, about that lady who follows me—are you being honest? You didn't hire her? She was at the Nowhere Club last Friday night."

"Well, I didn't invite her," Courtney added defensively.

The papers had blared—CHILD STAR BREAKS UP

BRAWL. The publicity for the TV film was so good that they were using less advertising and Courtney had gotten better billing.

"But, Cathy, I've tried to tell you—she really *is* following you! You have to believe me!"

I shook my head. "But why would anyone follow me? And what should I do?"

Courtney stared at the ceiling, thinking. "I know. Let's go for a walk and see if we can catch her following you and then we'll ask her."

Courtney logic. Well, I thought, maybe it would work.

As we went down in the elevator, I said, "Now, let me get this straight. We're looking for someone who's looking for me but we don't know why."

"Nope," Courtney said. "See, someone is following you, and we are going to follow her to see why she is following you."

There was a woman in the elevator with a shopping cart full of laundry who looked as if she might want to interrupt and ask questions.

I could feel the familiar butterflies begin to flutter when we were out on the street. Were we going to get into trouble again? I didn't think I could take one more episode—I wasn't getting any younger.

"Cathy," Courtney suddenly hissed, sending chills up my spine. "There she is, the Mystery Lady."

I looked across the street. Sure enough it was her. This time she had on a wide straw hat with a white brim and black crown and oversize black sunglasses. She was wearing a white suit and carrying a black patent leather clutch bag. She looked like a 1940s movie star.

"It's now or never, Cath," Courtney said, perking up for a little action.

Make it never, I thought. I suddenly felt scared and didn't want to know why the Mystery Woman was on my trail.

"Let's run down Seventy-ninth Street and duck into a building or behind some parked cars and then pop out and chase her like they do in the movies," Courtney said breathlessly. "She'll never get that far in those heels."

Locked into another adventure with my crazy cousin Courtney, but this time it was my adventure.

Courtney bent down and straightened her sock, and then we began to run as fast as we could. We ducked into the lobby of a building without a doorman, then peeked out the door. The Mystery Lady was right behind us, wobbling on her heels. Too bad she couldn't find a job. This couldn't have paid very well.

"*Now,* Cathy!" We ran out of the building with Courtney saying, "It's now or never!"

We ran straight up to her and stopped.

The woman knew she was caught. Her big sunglasses slipped down to her nose. Courtney pulled herself up with every inch of her do-good, self-righteousness, help-the-underdog outrage and said in a very loud voice, "What has *my* cousin *done* to you!"

Two old ladies stopped as if they anticipated a street fight.

The woman said nothing at first, but she knew her time was up.

"Nothing, nothing," she murmured. "I was hired to do this."

I was glad she was being paid. She had been working hard at it.

She gave us her card. It had a palm tree on it and said EARTHQUAKE DETECTIVE AGENCY, LOS ANGELES, LYDIA PINKERTON.

"I was hired by Liam DeMille," she said.

"Oh," Courtney said.

Great. That explained everything.

"Who's Liam DeMille?" we both asked at once.

"Liam DeMille is your father," she said to me.

I mumbled something unintelligible. My father? My dad was this long-ago disappeared actor who called himself Cliff Carleton instead of Cliff Bushwick. I didn't hate him, because I knew he had a dream to follow, and that dream was to be an actor, well, a movie star.

"He made it!" Lydia said, throwing her hands high into the air. "He has a major picture coming out. He wanted me to tell you before you saw him on a talk show."

"But why have you been following me?" I wanted to know. "Why didn't you just tell me?"

"Your dad knows he's been a lousy father, and he wants to try to change that. He hired me to follow you to gather as much information about you as possible before he contacts you. He really wanted to know the nitty-gritty details of your life, and that meant I had to follow you for a long time. You gave him a lot of laughs. He always thought you were such a serious kid."

This sounded weird to me, but who knows with actors? I mean, look at Courtney. She's an actor, and heaven knows she's weird. I guess I understood it—kind of.

"See, he always cared about you, but he could barely take care of himself," Lydia continued.

I could see Courtney crying. She was romantic.

Lydia started to cry then, too. I could see the tears under her large-size sunglasses. I felt confused and I wasn't about to cry then. Maybe later when I'd had the time to sort everything out. How do you feel inside when something like this happens? I guess I felt a mixture of emotions, which was very hard for me.

Courtney handed Lydia a Kleenex.

Lydia was actually sobbing now. "What do you say, Cathy, can you give him a second chance?"

I kind of nodded. Actually I couldn't remember my dad. Only one thing about him came to mind.

He was fun. Like Courtney. Like an actor. In fact, he was like a large child. I smiled.

"Tell him to call me," I said.

Courtney and Lydia clapped me on the back.

I was still confused.

I never really thought of myself as having a father. Not in the sense other girls do. Howard was wonderful, but he wasn't my dad.

Out of the clear blue I asked, "How did you get off so easy?"

"I beg your pardon?"

"At the Nowhere Club the other evening. You were nowhere to be found."

"Oh, that. Well, I'm a private eye. I told them I was following you. By the way, your father liked that one, Cathy. He loves you."

I wish she'd stop saying—your father. I hadn't thought of him that way in years. Now everything wasn't black and white. It was a mess.

As the Mystery Woman walked away, Courtney said, "Cheer up Cath. You'll get more stuff this way."

CHAPTER THIRTEEN

During the last weeks of summer vacation Rock broke the habit. He came by with four Dinosaurs, then three, then two, and then one day, as Courtney squealed, he came up alone. Courtney, Rock, Frank, and I went everywhere together except to the Nowhere Club.

No one could be like Frank.

Ever.

I was having a wonderful time, but I was also counting the days off on my calendar. He was going back to Idaho, and I was going to be staying in New York.

"Long-distance relationships never work," Courtney said sadly.

Courtney felt the same way about Rock. He was going back to England. But she expressed it differently. She moped around the house like some actress from a late-night movie.

"Come on, Courtney," I said, trying to cheer her up. "You'll get another boyfriend." She wasn't even fourteen yet, and she had more boyfriends than her age.

We were both emotional messes about Frank and Rock leaving.

We still went to Camp Acorn, of course. Zora Zimmerman had a new bribe—tuna fish salad sandwiches. She was writing a new book about the Civil War called *First Shot at Love*.

Mostly I just felt so discombobulated.

And I hated that.

I thought about my dad and wondered how and when I would meet him. How would I feel?

I knew I liked Frank a lot, but I also knew I was excited about starting school. Fresh notebooks, new pens and pencils. I wanted to play the viola in the school orchestra. I always loved the first day of school.

Courtney didn't want to go back to school at all.

One afternoon Courtney and I were sitting on our beds. She was biting her lip and trying to choose the best publicity shot of her, and I was trying to read her parts of *My Crazy Cousin Courtney Returns Again,* when the phone rang.

We both scrambled for it.

"It's probably Rock!" she screeched.

113

"It could be Frank!"

We bumped into each other and picked up the phone together, sharing the receiver.

It was my mom.

I could hear her yelling in the background, "Scottie, tell the director the giraffe isn't too tall!"

"Listen, Cathy and Courtney, Howard and I want to take you to Hung Lo's tonight for a farewell dinner."

Neither of us said anything. No fortune cookie could bring us good news. Frank and Rock were leaving soon, and we wanted to be with them—not with my mom and Howard.

We hung up the phone. My mom had said to meet them at six. "Oh, Cathy," Courtney said, flopping down on her bed. "What'll we do? These have been some of the best weeks of my life. I shall never forget—"

"Courtney, maybe we should get ready," I said. I cut her short because I didn't want to get sadder still.

That evening at dinner I ate only the wontons from the soup and played with my *moo goo gai pan*. I could see Courtney was doing the same thing, and she loved to eat.

My mom smiled at us and took out two quarters from her bag. "Okay, girls, why don't you call Rock and Frank and see if they can meet you for ice cream."

Courtney and I crashed into each other and almost knocked over the table.

There was a payphone in the back.

We picked up the receiver together and then started to fight over it.

"You call first."

"No. You call first," Courtney said.

Finally we flipped a quarter. I had heads and Courtney had tails.

Frank was in and said he could come.

Then Courtney called Rock. He didn't have a phone, but he lived upstairs from a Laundromat, and they let him know when he had a call.

This would be the last night all four of us could be together—Rock had to work at the Nowhere Club the next night, and Frank had to have a farewell dinner with his grandmother and visit his New York cousins. Courtney was leaving first, then Frank, then Rock. I told Frank about the Mystery Woman, but I never told him it was an almost lie.

Courtney wouldn't let me.

"Who knows when I'll ever see Rock again?" Courtney said that night after our last magical evening, a big bubble bursting all over her face. Courtney was cracking me up because she had begun acting like a heroine in a Civil War movie. It rubbed off on her from Zora, who was in her Civil war phase à la her book.

Courtney picked the gum from her face. Suddenly

115

I could see Courtney Green all grown up in a stunning black strapless gown accepting her Oscar award and picking bubble gum off her face while she thanked Bernie and Joan and her agent and Wilheim Von Dog.

Then she stopped being melodramatic and said, "Who knows when I'll ever see *you* again?"

She had said it first.

We were both quiet.

"Courtney," I said. "I feel like we're sisters."

"Yep," she said.

"A little of you rubbed off on me and a little of me rubbed off on you."

"Yep," she said. I could see her mysterious blue-green eyes getting misty.

"Will you write to me?" I asked.

"Yep."

I knew she wouldn't.

The Big Day came too soon. Courtney was packed (well, she hadn't really unpacked all that much) and ready to go. She had eleven baggage claims, which she held like a pack of cards, one carry-on case with her bubble gum, and a doggie cage that said, "Free Wilheim Von Dog."

All of us had gone to JFK airport to say goodbye to her. Frank, Rock, Mrs. Phillips, who was now dating the producer, who was interested in Courtney for a film that promised to be an award-winner.

"Remember, Courtney, it won't be so bad without Rock. You're a big movie star now. When your movie comes out, everyone will be wanting to meet you," I advised hopefully.

"Oh, Cathy," she said. "You're always trying to take care of me. You know that's not true. I'll feel bad about not seeing Rock." Then she added, "But I feel good about being a movie star. Who wouldn't?"

That left me all alone and no movie star. Frank would be leaving for Idaho the next day for good, and I would only have my pens and notebooks and a shiny viola.

"Courtney," I said while the passengers were starting to board, "you'll always be my best friend."

Courtney hugged me. If it was possible, she had grown even prettier over the summer. "I feel the same way, Cath," she said. "We'll always be the best of friends no matter where we are."

I could see my mom taking a Kleenex out of her bag. "Your mother and I said the same thing to each other when we were about your age."

And then Courtney kissed everyone, and she and Rock hugged, which was pretty funny because Rock was about a head taller than she was. But he came without the Dinosaurs, which was good.

I knew then as I watched a big cherry bubble burst all over her face that no matter how far away Courtney might be, she would never really be that far.

About the Author

JUDI MILLER was brought up in Cleveland, Ohio, but writes and lives in New York City. She is the author of *My Crazy Cousin Courtney* and *My Crazy Cousin Courtney Comes Back*, both available from Minstrel Books. Judi, who has liked to write since she was nine years old, also writes suspense thrillers for adults.